U.S. Copyright: TXu 2-313-366

ISBN: 979-8-636609120-6 (Paperback)

Any reference to historical events, real people, or real places are used fictitiously. Names, characters, and places are products of the author's imagination.

Front Cover page by MUniqueDesign

1

Phoneless?

I stepped off the bus to finally smell the freshness of afterschool freedom, with my thirteen-year-old big brother Dontay right behind me. I stuffed my hands into my pockets and braced for the whiff of air from the bus whirring past us before we crossed the street to head home.

"Clay, I told you all that mouthin' you do to your teachers would catch up to you. K gon' be hot with you, bro!" Tay said.

I frowned and rolled my eyes at his words. I had finally taken in some fresh air without a teacher in sight, and school was the last thing I wanted to think about. While I knew I had been dumb at school that day, I was not ready to admit it to my brother, who always felt the need to remind me of how dumb I could be. I was worried about what our oldest brother Kemis would say or do when he found out what happened, knowing he was tired of hearing from the school about my behavioral troubles. Or even worse, I wondered if Kemis would ask Pastor D, the youth pastor from church, to come talk to me and "save me" from being bad.

"Bro, I ain't think she heard me. I wasn't trying to say it that loud!" It was the only reply I had, but I knew I'd have to think of something better before I got home. Tay knew it too.

"You better figure out what you gon' tell him. Getting another F is bad enough. But followed up with that? And another detention? You been getting detention like every week! Dude, you done," he said, shaking his head.

I began brainstorming, wondering if I could tell Kemis my head was hurting, or that I hadn't slept well the night before, or that I missed Granny. In that moment, I wished Jason, our second oldest brother, was actually the oldest. Jason was seventeen, a senior in high school, and we could confess to him even our most terrible deeds without him losing his temper. Not only could we tell him everything, but he told us nearly everything too. He even told us things Kemis wouldn't want him telling us about, like his dealings with all of his girlfriends. But Jason wasn't the one I would have to face regarding another write-up at school, and I knew Kemis would not be happy once he heard about it.

"Yo, throw my bag on my bed," I told Tay once we crossed the parking lot and arrived at our front stoop.

His eyes grew wide and his voice louder. "Where you going? You know K gon' be looking for you when he gets home," he said.

"I'm just going up to the court for a minute. Once he finds out what I did, you know he ain't gon' let me out. It's gon' be quick!"

Tay looked at me and shook his head, knowing I had a terrible idea, and knowing my trips to the basketball court were never quick.

"Bro," he said, "you need to at least start your homework. He was on one the other day 'cause he said you keep leaving without your work done, and you ain't been turning your homework in at school."

Tay was always annoyingly reciting Kemis' rules about homework that only seemed to apply to me. I hated homework and anything else that kept me inside, especially when the weather was nice, and the sun stayed out longer. I was my best self when I was outside in the sunlight, especially if I was with my boys at the basketball court. I generally ignored my brother's words to go hoop, willing and ready to face his wrath later.

This day would be no different. I didn't want to be stuck in the house, and I needed time to generate a plausible excuse for my indiscretions at school that day. I headed down the sidewalk and quickly picked up the pace before Tay could get louder and inadvertently alert Jason and Daveon, our other brothers, of my departure.

"It'll be quick, I promise!" I yelled and jetted along, already past the apartment unit next door.

As usual, my time at the basketball court turned out to not be so quick. The fellas had just started a game and invited me to join in once I walked through the chain-link fence that enclosed the basketball court. As was typical, one game turned to eight or nine, and soon the streetlights were illuminating our scrimmage, with the moonlight assisting. I had completely forgotten about school, other than a joke that Jon, who was in class when it all went down, cracked about the day's events.

"Bruh straight up. I lowkey can't stand that teacher!" I said while another player was off retrieving the ball.

"Can't nobody stand her! Bet yo' brotha gon' be pissed!" Terrell said.

"Ain't nobody trippin' off him. I'm runnin' thangs, bruh!" I said, trying my best to sound convincing.

"Nigga you ain't say that when he smacked yo' ass that time at the court!" Jon said.

"Naw, that was his granny. I remember that shit, bruh. We was out here dying!" Terrell said while laughing.

"How bout y'all niggas focus on playin' some D instead'a my granny," I said, trying to change the subject.

"Yo' black ass need to focus on some new shoes to ball in," Josh said, causing them to look at my feet, which displayed worn black sneakers with tattered laces and pealed fabric that Kemis had picked up from a thrift shop.

"Whatever nigga. Yo' shoes new and you still getting yo' ankles broke tryna guard me!"

Trash talk was a regular part of our time at the court, but Josh knew I was telling the truth. I was a fierce competitor and played better than most of my friends and a lot of older kids, even though I was playing on an empty stomach since we had played through dinner time.

Just before I was about to check ball at another game point, Jon motioned to the parking lot next to the basketball court. "What's yo' brother doing here?"

While I had slipped away intentionally, I had not meant to stay so late as to cause my oldest brother to come looking for me. He usually sent one of the others for that purpose unless he was really mad. I had lost track of time and forgotten that my whole reason for coming was to stall our confrontation and come up with a new excuse for why I had gotten into trouble at school again. Instead, I had gotten lost in the basketball games and had forgotten that my life would be hanging in the balance once the principal called my house, or likely, my brother's cell phone.

I had forgotten that I hadn't done homework and I hadn't come straight home like I was supposed to. I also had forgotten that I would be facing the look that was on my brother's face in that moment, that look that expressed that I was lucky there were laws against killing younger brothers. He was standing outside of his truck, on the passenger's side, with his arms crossed, silently glaring at me and our game, the way he often did when he was unhappily dragging me from my happy place.

"Ay y'all, I gotta go," I said with a defeated tone.

"You must ain't talked to him about school yet," Jon said.

"Finish this game, nigga! Tell him you running thangs!" Josh said with a smirk.

I shook my head at him. "I'll holla at y'all later," I said as I grabbed my shirt and phone off the bench and strolled over to the truck, where Kemis opened the passenger door for me in silence.

As expected, it was a bad ride home. He didn't exactly yell at me but projected at the level right beneath a full-blown yell.

"Clay, this is crazy. I seriously don't even have words. First of all, you get in trouble at school *again* and you decide to go play basketball instead of bringing yo' tail home like you supposed to! How many times have I told you to get your stuff done before you go over to that basketball court?" he asked.

I looked down at my lap. I knew he'd be mad about that one.

"And then instead of studying for your test like you're supposed to, you decide to be dumb enough to cheat and get caught? And then instead of owning up to your mistake like a middle schooler should be mature enough to do, you cuss out your teacher?" he continued.

"I ain't cuss her out!" I didn't think one cuss word constituted a whole "cussing out." It was an unfair and exaggerated description of my verbal exchange, I thought.

"I talked to your teacher. Don't play me. I know exactly what you said. Bro, I promise you I could drop kick you into next week. Your mouth outta hand, lil' bro. And not only that, all the answers to the test were in the study guide. Had you just read through it a couple of times when I told you to study you would've been fine! But you wanna sneak off to hoop or play games or find your friends! Your friends ain't gon' help you pass the seventh grade, bro! In fact, it looks like they gon' help you fail it!" he yelled.

It was a talk we had repeatedly before, about how I knew better than the way I was behaving, how I was caving into peer pressure and heading down a broad, dangerous path. I considered it as simply getting caught cheating on a stupid science test, and I didn't know what path he was talking about.

"Bro, if Granny was alive, she'd be paddling yo' lil' tail right now!" he added.

She definitely did a lot of that, second only to my brother Daveon, who actually did complete a full cussing out of some of his teachers. I had always admired him for being better at it than me. His disrespectful words flowed smoothly and eloquently, like in a scene from the movies. I figured if I kept practicing I would one day sound as natural as he did.

Kemis continued in his tongue lashing while I longed to be back at the basketball court. I was annoyed that I was being talked at, and as usual, I didn't get a chance to speak—not that I had anything to say in defense of my actions. I knew it was wrong when my friend Terrell had somehow come across the answers to the quiz we were taking, and he held up his paper so I could copy down all the right answers. Getting the answers from him was much easier than studying and the only way to guarantee a good grade.

Someone must've snitched because the teacher stormed right over and snatched up both of our papers and sent us to the office, which was when I mouthed off and allowed profanity to slip out. I had my reasons for letting it slip, but they were reasons I knew Kemis wouldn't accept. She was the same teacher that had once told me in the hallway that I wouldn't "amount to anything." I could still picture watching her tilted glasses, coffee-stained teeth, and cracked lips utter the words as she said it. I remembered wanting someone like the principal to know about it, but I knew he wouldn't have believed it coming from me anyway, and she knew it too.

Kemis reminded me that I had cheated on the same quiz that he repeatedly told me to study for, and every time I was supposed to be studying, he caught me outside with my boys or playing video games. He told me I wasn't going out, couldn't have anyone over, and I was banned from video games until I earned a better grade. There was to be no internet or computer, unless it was for school. He continued lecturing and pronouncing my punishments while we sat in the truck in front of the apartment. I looked down or out the window, making clear my disinterest in his monologue, yearning for it to finally end.

When he finally ended his speech, it was with words that no kid wanted to hear: "Now go ahead and run me that cell phone."

I wanted to throw it at him, but the last time he told me to give him my phone I actually did throw it, and he got up and tackled me. I figured I wasn't going that route anymore and I shifted over in my seat to pull my phone out of my pocket and dropped it in the center console, keeping my eyes out the front window.

"Go to your room and don't come out until your work is done. I'll bring you up some food in a lil' bit. You hear me?" he asked.

"Yeah whatever," I said. I threw open the door of the truck and went inside, upstairs to my room, slamming the door behind me.

I grumbled as I got out my backpack, wishing I didn't have to overhear my brothers playing video games in the other room. I was jealous that they had all finished their homework and were free to spend the evening how they chose. I instead had an un-fun plan to hurry up and do boring work and go to sleep…except, I didn't do the boring work at all.

I dozed off, dreaming about my teacher, the scowl on her face, and the face of the classmate that must have snitched me out for cheating. I dreamt I was walking down the street and they were riding by in a drop-top car, pointing and laughing at me. Everyone else on the street was laughing and pointing too. I was mad watching them laugh and had started to chase the car to pound them both down when I was awakened by the unpleasant feeling and sound effects of Kemis catching me sleeping.

Whap! Whap!

"Whoa, bro! Chill!" I pled, wanting him to stop hitting me with my flip flop. I tried to turn and block while offering an explanation.

"Bro! It was an accident! I was doing this dumb ass ma—"
Whap! Whap! Whap!

"Shit, bro!" I yelled. The words were already out when I realized I needed them back in.

He glared at me. "So you just gon' cuss at me like you do your teachers? I told you to come in here and do your work! This is exactly why you weren't ready for that test today. I tell you to come study or do homework and you drift off into something else! You supposed to sleep at night, but instead you sneak downstairs and watch tv all night or sneak on yo' phone! You twelve years old, bro! You know better than to do this stuff!" Kemis said.

While I knew I was supposed to do my work, keeping my brain on task was much harder than just knowing what was expected. Sleeping at night had become increasingly difficult, and the tv was the only thing that would help me ignore my own brain long enough to fall asleep. And even with watching television, my sleep was choppy and inconsistent, and dozing off during the day had become routine.

His muscular frame sank down next to me on top of my blanket, and he bent forward with his head in his hands while he lightly bounced his right foot up and down on the floor. I could sense his fatigue and frustration with me by the way he stared at the floor through the openings in his fingers, in between closing his eyes and taking deep breaths. I also knew his brain was nothing like mine, and he would never be able to understand me.

My brother was naturally intelligent and excelled at school, something I had never done. At some point during high school, he decided he wanted good grades, and he raised his grades up without help from anyone other than Pastor D and his wife. He went on to graduate near the top of his high school class. Granny had been so proud since he was only the second one in the entire family to get a high school diploma. He had been offered a full scholarship to nearly every college he applied after his counselor at school had helped him fill out applications and get his application fees waived since Granny couldn't afford to pay them. He took a scholarship to a local community college instead, and took most of his classes online, in addition to working full-time to help Granny pay the bills. He was also working to become a certified fitness trainer, and was taking classes in Krav Maga, an Israeli martial art. He was handsome and talented and smart, a naturally resourceful hustler, and I had long given up on trying to be like him, despite the fact that I admired everything about him.

It turned out to be fortunate that he had stayed around with us, since he was the best candidate to become our legal guardian after Granny passed away. We had a useless mother and fathers we didn't often talk about, and each of us had individual needs of our own that probably only Kemis would have known how to handle. Being ten years older than me, I couldn't help but wonder how often he regretted the fact that he agreed to parent us full-time, considering all the other things he was talented at.

He slid his arm on top of my shoulder, reminding me of when he had tried to comfort me when Granny had passed away eight months before. I recalled our final moments with her, when she had been in the kitchen downstairs, sitting at the table, talking with Tay about one of his classmates at school while she peeled potatoes and Tay worked alongside her on his iPad. But it was the longest night ever, starting with when she clutched her chest and crashed onto the floor, until hours later when we were waiting to hear from Kemis about her condition, and Jason telling us we needed to go to bed and get ready for school.

But we didn't go to school that next morning or the next few mornings. Our whole world had crashed, and school was the last thing we cared about. Kemis unsuccessfully tried to convince us we needed to return to school after nearly a week off, but it took some nudging from Pastor D, who reminded us that the social worker wouldn't look favorably on a guardianship plan if we weren't listening to Kemis and regularly attending school.

I had hardly had even one decent night's sleep since she left us. The flashbacks were almost constant, and every time the lights went out, my nightly companion—anxiety—greeted me as I anticipated another night of insomnia.

"I worry about y'all. I worry about you getting kicked out of school and attracted to street life. It's crazy because Granny was so proud when she was able to make a little more money to get us in this apartment complex and away from the old neighborhood. Then Pastor D helped her get each of you your own bed…she just knew things would be better here. Little did she know this neighborhood would get nearly as bad as the old one.

"Look, bro, I don't want you to feel like I'm comparing you to Tay, but I know you're smart too. I get it that you have some challenges, but your grades and these behavior reports don't reflect what you're capable of. For real, what's up with you and school?" he asked.

"K, I'm not smart…and I hate school. Why can't I just stay home and learn? The celebrity kids learn at home with tutors," I said.

He sighed. "Tutors cost money, baby bro. Do you know how broke we are?"

"Actually yes. The kids at school remind me every fucking day, and you remind me every time I ask for something that costs more than a dolla," I told him. It sucked when it seemed like everyone else had expensive shoes, name brand clothing, or clothes that didn't all come from the closets of older brothers.

"Watch your mouth. Most of them are broke too, Clay. If they weren't, I guarantee they wouldn't live in our neighborhood. When people over here get a little money, the first thing they do is move. These kids over here just hide it better because every now and then someone buys them some nice shoes, or their mama gets a tax refund...that's not real money. You know I would love to be able to do those things for you. Maybe next year after I finish school and get a better job I can. For now, I try to at least make sure you have some shoes you can hoop in, but I can't afford to get you the latest stuff all the time. But don't listen to them kids at school, and who cares what they think if they're not even your friends."

"Even my friends talk about my clothes."

"Then they ain't yo' friends! And they on assistance just like us! I know it's hard right now, but one day and you ain't even gon' be thinking 'bout these kids like that. Plus, y'all are healthy, smart, athletic, no major problems; we gotta count our blessings."

I couldn't understand why he always called me smart when he knew I wasn't. I could hardly focus on a two-page study guide long enough to prepare for a test, let alone be able to explain a math problem or finish one of my assigned readings. Even with the guidance counselor giving me labels that Granny never wanted me to have, I could still tell that my teachers knew that even with extra time and help, I couldn't perform like my peers, and definitely not like some of my brothers.

I was sure that what he said made sense in his own brain, but it didn't do much for me. I was tired of always feeling like the dumb kid in class and the broke kid at school, and him telling me to count my blessings didn't alleviate any of the feelings I was having.

"At the end of the day, Clay, you gotta do better. I know it's hard trying to figure out how to adjust to life without Granny. And just because you hate school doesn't mean you don't do what you're supposed to do. I'm taking this Economics class that I absolutely hate, so I have to put in even more effort than normal to keep my grade up! That's a part of being responsible."

"Yeah, but people making money on IG and YouTube just by posting videos and you taking a class you ain't gon' use!"

"Not everybody can make money like that just by getting followers. Just like not everybody going to the NBA or NFL. Most of us just gotta figure out how to find happiness in our everyday lives. Right now, I gotta figure out how to keep food on the table and keep the rent paid while I get y'all and me through school."

He continued lecturing and then transitioned into sharing funny stories about Granny, including one when she got on him after he was caught throwing cheese out the window while eating lunch during an in-school suspension. After we finished joking and laughing, he said a prayer, something he did a lot more after Granny died.

"I love you baby bro," he told me as he got up and headed towards the door. "And don't think you gon' sneak and take yo' phone before school like you did last time you were on punishment. It's not even going down like that."

I rolled my eyes thinking how much I hated not having my phone or video games, especially at school when my friends were playing on their phones or talking about the games that they had played together, or the videos they had sent each other and watched the night before. Our video games and our group text chats were the main things we had in common, and I felt isolated when I couldn't discuss them. I hoped I would be able to bring up my grade with my next Science quiz so I could regain some sliver of a social life and feel like a part of the crew again. Otherwise, I needed a plan to make money and buy my own phone that wasn't controlled by my brother.

2

HANG TIME

I didn't know if it was normal that my friends had such a huge influence on the things that I did, especially when their home lives were nothing like mine.

Despite what all the teachers and security officers at school said about our crew, my friends and I weren't necessarily bad kids, but we didn't have a positive influence on each other. We did a lot of things we knew we shouldn't in the name of impressing one another. We often came up with bad ideas, and egged each other on instead of trying to talk one another out of getting into trouble.

In the sixth grade, Jon took his deceased grandfather's car for a spin after finding the keys hidden in a drawer in his mom's bedroom. He drove that beat-down car everywhere, including to the basketball court where Terrell and I were in a game. We congratulated him for getting there without any accidents and stood around talking and laughing outside the car, daring him to make additional stops.

"Does yo' mama know you got this?" Terrell asked with a smirk. Jon didn't answer, but only laughed and told us to get in with him.

"Dude, you crazy!" I told him, which I think he actually liked hearing.

We were silly enough to ride with him to the house of a girl we knew from school, who was hanging outside with her friends. We kept daring him to drive to different places and got a kick out of watching the reactions of other motorists that would pass us by, most of whom looked on in shock at seeing our young faces. We couldn't believe we made it so far without any police interaction. It made us popular that week, having been seen riding around with Jon.

He got caught a few weeks later and stopped coming to get us, after he returned home one day after driving to see a girl and found his mom waiting for him on their front stoop. He said she started hitting him as soon as he got out the car, but he ran into his room and locked the door. I remembered sharing the story with Daveon and Tay, who both told me I was crazy for getting in the car with an eleven-year-old driver.

Josh's mom and Jon's mom usually worked odd shifts, so the two of them would hang out all day and make it home before their mothers did, which sometimes would not be until after midnight. Terrell's grandma worked a lot too, and he would usually just tell her he was at my house when she inquired about his whereabouts, even though he hardly ever was. Since the three of them could often hang out at places and times that I couldn't, the only times I could feel like a full member of the crew was at school and at the basketball court. I desperately wanted more outings with them, but they didn't understand what it was like to have four older brothers like I did, all of whom at points acted like they were in charge of me.

"Clay, you gotta come to Terron's party Friday night. His momma not gon' be home. I heard his brother say he getting' lit! He said it's gon' be hella girls there too," Josh said. We were hanging out near our lockers after our first class, the week after my detention.

"Yeah, bruh! Jamisa and her whole crew said they coming!" Jon said.

"My brother gon' say no since I'm still on punishment," I said.

"Dude, yo' brother be having you on punishment for like ten years for some bullshit! That time you went home hella late over the summer, we ain't see you for like a month! Nigga gon' be eighteen by the time you can come out," said Terrell.

Terrell was almost right—the crew and I had a wild night over the summer, so wild that I stayed out later to keep my brother from sensing all the substances that were in my body. He told me I couldn't go outside for three weeks, which I would do anyway when he would leave. It had only been a week this time, but Kemis had already emphasized that he wasn't letting me off the hook until I took and passed the next science quiz.

"Clay, errrrbody gon' be at this party, bruh. Only the lames are staying home. Just sneak out yo' brothers' window and meet us there!" said Jon, who always had the best and worst ideas.

Josh always agreed with the others if it meant pressuring one of us to do something, no matter how outlandish the idea. "Yeah man, remember that time I climbed up there and spent the night with you and Tay?" he asked. I recalled what had been a fun, unexpected evening where Tay spent all night telling us to keep quiet so Kemis didn't get suspicious. Josh had been hanging with some girl but had told his mom he was at his dad's house and couldn't return home until the morning.

Jason and Daveon had used their window as a third entryway and exit from the apartment since their early teens. The large second-floor window let out over a large brick portico over the front door and front porch near a tree. They had taught their guests how to scale it with prowess. Years before when Granny was allowed to get an alarm installed on the apartment after a series of break-ins in the area, coming in late and sneaking out were no longer options for the two of them, bringing their normal schedule to an abrupt halt. The alarm was attached to all the downstairs windows and doors, but the two of them were ecstatic to find that the upstairs windows were not attached to the alarm system, and were back to business as usual.

With a gateway to the party, I spent the rest of the day imagining myself increasing my popularity by hanging out late with the popular kids and partying with my friends and other kids from school, and wondering how I would get Tay to go along with my plan. While Tay got into trouble every now and then, he was more level-headed and generally made better choices than me. Since he was with me the most, he carried the burden of trying to keep me from doing something stupid to keep us both out of trouble with Kemis. I knew I would need Jason and Daveon on my side in order to get Tay on board.

Kemis was still working at his desk with his headset on when we arrived home from school, giving me the opportunity to sail past him and start working on my plan.

"What up, fellas!" he called before quickly returning to a phone call. "Actually, the account was negative at the time of the withdrawal…"

"Sup bro!" we greeted before taking off upstairs.

I missed the days before he started working from home when we could sneak around with friends after school or have some friends over before completing homework. It was likely some of those things that prompted him to seek the job that allowed him to be home when we arrived.

While Jason's rigorous basketball schedule became more manageable after he was able to drive himself around, it was Daveon's behavior that caused us the most lifestyle changes. On our very first day back at school after Granny died, Daveon was suspended for three weeks for punching another student in the face so hard that he broke his jaw. He beat down another student nearly a week within returning from his suspension, and the police took him to the juvenile court.

Soon, he was regularly skipping school and leaving school early to go hang with his boys until late into the night, not telling any of us where he was or what he was doing. All of Daveon's drama caught up with him one night when the police brought him home for the third time in just a few months, prompting Kemis to scrounge up money to send him away to a lengthy summer camp out of state.

With Daveon's history, I knew my brothers wouldn't want to offer a lot of support for my idea of sneaking out to a late party, but I was desperate to attend. I threw my backpack in my room and went to find Jason and Daveon with a mission to get them on my side. With Jason having the day off from basketball practice, the two of them were lounging in their room listening to music while completing their assignments from school. Daveon had a workbook open but was on his phone texting. Jason, who was much more diligent about his work since his basketball coach made them turn it in, looked as though he was actually tending to homework.

"Sup, young C," Jason greeted me while Daveon remained silent, smiling and looking at his phone, which was cupped in his hand. I looked around to make sure no one was coming and quietly closed the door behind me. I sized up the window in their room, which occupied the space in between their beds.

I spoke in a low voice as I crept in and sat down on Day's bed. "Yo I gotta ask y'all something, and don't—"

"Bro, if you got suspended or detention again, don't come crying in here when K kick yo' ass! You need to start doing yo' work and get out that daggone remedial reading class," Daveon blurted out. He was always one for being brutally honest and cutting to the chase, and always annoyingly assuming the worst.

"It ain't even like that! I ain't get in trouble at school today. I'm not doing that no more anyway," I said.

"Yeah, you say that shit all the time but okay," he responded. I rolled my eyes in annoyance with his words.

Jason cut in, "Bro, just let him talk. W'sup?" He had turned around from his desk, signaling that I had his undivided attention.

"Terron havin' this lil' party Friday night." They were already giving me that look after I uttered the word "party," the look with an eyebrow raised and their lips formed into a frown. I continued anyway, wishing I hadn't started with the party. "K ain't gon' let me go and—"

"What kinda party?" Daveon asked suspiciously.

"Just a little party at his crib! It's just—"

"The last time I took one of y'all somewhere while y'all were on punishment, I ended up on punishment, bro. Ain't happening," Jason said.

I retorted, "Damn! Can I just finish? Y'all never let me talk!" They settled down and let me finish pleading my case. "I don't need a ride anywhere. I can walk. The only way I can do it is if I go out through the window in here. I just wanna go for a lil' bit. I ain't gon' be gone all night," I said.

Jason started rubbing his forehead like the notion stressed him out. Daveon's expression hadn't changed—he still looked at me like I was crazy.

"C'mon, don't act like y'all don't be using the window to get out too, and we always cover for y'all," I reminded them.

Jason broke his silence. "What's Tay gon' say if K ask him where you at? What if he catches you coming in or out the window? Besides, you only twelve. You don't need to be out late like that," he said.

I hadn't covered all those details yet. I was just relying on my hope that none of the scenarios he had posed would happen. "I haven't asked him yet, but I can get him to cover for me. It's not like he gon' snitch!" I said, proving I had a plan. Snitching was something the four of us never did, as we had made a no-snitch pact years ago that had been tested and tried repeatedly, even during dire circumstances. "And why y'all be acting like y'all never snuck out at twelve?"

"I don't know, man. K having company this Friday. If he catch you, he gon' kee-ill all of us, but especially me. The fall dance is coming up in a couple weeks, and I can't be out here with no keys," Jason said.

He knew he had made a solid point, and Daveon silently nodded in agreement. I definitely didn't want his keys taken away since the fact that he was driving was a benefit we all enjoyed. Still, I couldn't give up that easily.

"Look, all my friends will be there, and I hardly ever get to go to anything they're at since K don't like them. There's no way I'ma get caught going out the window. I've practiced it like a hundred times! Besides, I only want to stop in for a lil' while, just like one hour, and I'll be right back home. I ain't going to Rel house or nowhere else, I promise."

"Lil' bro, I know exactly where that dude live. You don't need to be over there by yoself—they probably gon' be getting high, and K gon' kill you if you come home smelling like weed again!" Daveon said.

"Day, I swear I ain't gon' smoke! I'm just saying what's up for a minute and leaving! I just want one hour!" I searched my brain for more ways to persuade them since neither of them looked convinced. "Y'all den snuck to hella parties! And girls' houses…and all kinds of other shit!"

After sighing and spending a moment staring at his phone, Jason finally responded in a favorable manner. "Forty-five minutes, bro, that's it. Otherwise I'ma come find you so you better watch the time. And I'm effing you up if I get in trouble," he warned harshly.

I knew he only agreed because of all the times Tay and I had covered for both of them. I couldn't count the times Kemis had left Jason in charge, and Jason dropped us off at the basketball court so he could see one of his girls. There were also those times he told Kemis he was taking us to the mall or the game, but actually dropped off Daveon to get high with his friends and dropped Tay and me at the movies or with friends so he could "get into some things." And of course, there had been at least a handful of times he and Daveon had snuck girls in while Kemis was at work or Granny was asleep. Tay and I would keep watch at the downstairs windows or at the top of the steps, ready to give the signal if one or both of them was about to be busted.

"You gon' have to take the burner in case we need to call you," he continued.

Jason had purchased a burner phone months before Granny passed away, a phone we could use when Kemis took ours as a part of punishment. It was something we had all used, although Tay rarely needed it, and Jason wasn't using it nearly as much as before. Between basketball, school, his part-time job at the library, and helping Kemis shuffle the rest of us around, he didn't have a whole lot of time for trouble.

"Big bro, I got you! I promise I ain't gon' get y'all in trouble!"

I ran out before Daveon could say something negative or before Jason could change his mind. My next and only goal was to convince Tay to go along with my plan. Unlike Jason and Daveon, Tay had never snuck out the house before. He was almost always where he said he was going to be, which was usually at school, the library, an after-school program, or playing video games with one of his friends.

I had always been convinced that he was Granny's favorite, and Kemis' too. Kemis trusted him, which was why I needed him on my side. He rarely told a lie, and if he did, it was usually to cover for one of us. The no-snitch policy we had between the four of us was hardest for Tay. He would never voluntarily tell on one of us, but under pressure he was the absolute worst liar.

He was lying down on his bed with his genius-level math workbook open, pencil in hand and headphones on when I walked in only somewhat admiring his work ethic.

"Yo, I gotta ask you something."

He already looked suspicious when I said it. Tay knew me better than anyone. There was only eleven months difference in our age even though he acted much older. We had shared everything when we were little—rooms, toys, clothes, beds, baths and showers. Now that we were older, we shared a room and almost always shared our thoughts. I knew which girls he liked, and he knew which bad decisions my friends had talked me into and where I would sneak off to with my friends after playing basketball. While we did everything together when we were younger, he had grown less interested in my escapades, and had become annoyed that I would make so many decisions that would land me, and often him, into trouble.

"Terron is having a party Friday night. I already know you gon' say I shouldn't do this, but I already talked Jay and Day into letting me sneak out their window. I just need you to cover if K ask you something," I said. I begged with my eyes, hoping he could get past the fact that I was still on punishment, and that generally every idea I ever had was terrible.

"Bro, you ain't even off punishment! You serious? And what you want me to say if K come in here actually looking for you, that you're in the bathroom or something?" asked Tay. He looked completely annoyed and had reacted that way I had expected.

"C'mon bro, I ain't gon' get caught! I'll prolly leave after midnight, after K think we sleep. And then I'll get back by one. Plus, he said he having a friend over that night. He not gon' be checking for me," I reasoned.

By now Tay was sitting up in his bed. He let out a long sigh, accompanied with an eye roll.

"Clay, you never think you gon' get—" He stopped his dissent when Kemis walked in and leaned his body against the dresser next to the doorway to speak to us, sounding and looking as though his day had been stressful. He always tried to interact and check in with us a little bit after school, something he told us the social worker recommended he do every day, even if he had been busy.

"W'sup y'all! Y'all have a good day?" he asked.

"Yeah," we responded in unison.

Tay broke the uncomfortable silence. "I got an A on my geography test," he said while faking a smile.

It was his norm. If he ever didn't get an A, he would freak out and act as though he was failing out of middle school. I secretly hated that my brother did so well since it made me feel like trash that I was running around cheating on tests while he excelled so naturally.

"Yoooo, that's what's up!" said Kemis as he dapped him up with a big smile. "Tay, I'm proud of you, lil' bro. We've had a lot of challenges this year, but you've really been a soldier and kept your head on straight."

He turned to me, "How was your day, C?"

He knew it wasn't likely I'd have any A's to report, unless it was from gym or art. He asked as though he actually wanted to know, and not like he had just gotten off the phone with one of my teachers. I hated those times when he would bait me and ask about my day, knowing he had already gotten a bad report and was just going to see if I would lie to him. But I had managed to remain trouble-free for the day, without a write-up or detention to report.

"Uh, it was cool," I tried to answer without raising any suspicions about anything. It seemed to work.

"Okay, well look I need to make a couple of quick calls," he said. "Get your work done, bro. Ay, when the last time you took a shower?" he asked me.

"Earlier…"

"Earlier today? Cause it smell like it was earlier this month!" he said.

"Why you always think it's me?" I asked.

"Cause it's usually you! Did you shower today?" he asked.

"Bro, I mean I washed and stuff!"

"As in, you stood at the sink and washed, but didn't actually get in the shower…Go take a shower when your homework done, bro. It shouldn't smell this bad in here," he said before backing out of the room. I was annoyed that he instructed only me to shower, but glad the coast was clear again so Tay and I could finish our discussion.

"Look Tay, I won't be gone long, and if I do get caught, all you gotta say is you were sleep and you didn't hear me leave. I'ma throw some pillows under my cover, and if he seems like he's about to come check on us, just turn out the lights and get in bed so he thinks we both sleep. You hardly have to do anything!" I said.

He finally agreed, but only on the condition that I agreed to no more sneak-outs for at least a year. He seemed tired of discussing it, but I was excited, and had convinced myself that the hardest part of my scheme was behind me.

3

SHE WAS WORTH IT

My nerves were in a frenzy that Friday night, and it was hard acting like everything was normal when I was secretly planning to pull off the scandal of the century. Despite my brain and body feeling like I was on a roller coaster ride, we were having a fairly typical Friday night in. Jason had returned from basketball practice and had thrown pizzas in the oven for dinner, which we all ate before helping Kemis clean up the front room for his guest. The four of us briefly introduced ourselves to Kemis' guest before we went upstairs, and Jason, Daveon, and Tay played video games while I mostly watched and plotted out my night. I took breaks to monitor Kemis' activities and make sure he remained occupied while mentally preparing for my departure.

My journey to the party was unexpectedly smooth. My boys were shocked to see me at the party, which made the sneak-out worth it for me. I felt like I was showing them that I was down with them.

Josh, who smelled like he had been smoking, said something first. "Big brother drill sergeant let you out?" He asked, prompting them all to chuckle.

"Man please," I responded, "you know I'm running things at the crib," I said with a smirk.

"Whateva nigga. We know you wouldn't say that in front of yo' brother. But look who here!" Josh gestured with his head across the room to the girl I was crushing on, Lakisha Smith.

We stood in one spot for a while talking and looking at each other's phones while watching other people in the party, but I mainly watched Lakisha. I wanted more than anything to touch her smooth coffee-colored skin and caress the dark curly hair that rested on her shoulders. I stared at her dimples every time she smiled, her teeth when she talked, and how she bounced her hips when she danced.

I wished I had the bravery and boldness of my older brothers to cross the room and throw my arms around her, tell her how much I wanted her as my girlfriend, and dance with her, but I was too afraid to do any of it. I became discouraged any time she talked with another boy. I had been reminded more times than I could count that she was too pretty for a dark and dusty boy like me—especially by Josh, who was used to getting most of the attention from girls at school. He had light skin with green eyes and wavy hair that he kept in a low cut, and I had always been jealous of the way girls geeked and gushed over him since our elementary school days.

Growing tired of watching me awkwardly stare, Terrell convinced me to go to talk to Lakisha. We weaved around a group of dancing kids to get to the back of the room while bobbing to the music that was loud enough to hear and enjoy, but low enough to keep the neighbors from calling the police.

Surveying the room from a new location allowed me to notice even more drinking and smoking than I was able to see from my original spot in the room. There was a couch with boys sitting down with girls on top of their laps, dancing along to the music or making out. Near the opposite wall were kids sitting on the steps who hardly left any room for the ones traversing up and down between the main floor and the upstairs bedrooms. It was mostly dark, other than a dim light coming from the kitchen area and the screens and lights from people's cell phones recording some of the madness.

Lakisha introduced Terrell to her cousin, and I nervously watched Terrell and the cousin walk away to talk while I happily but uncomfortably stood next to Lakisha. She ended the awkward silence that followed and soon we were talking about school while we people watched and laughed at other party goers and how wild some of them were being. I watched her lips every time she opened her mouth, and tried not to smile too hard every time she showed a sign that she was enjoying our conversation. She gave me her Snapchat and her number and told me I should text her when I got off punishment. I would've snuck out one hundred more times if I knew it meant I'd have her number by the end of the night.

I was relieved when she told me that she had lied to her mom to come to the party, telling her she would be at her cousin's house. She laughed in disbelief when I confessed to her that I had climbed out my brothers' window to sneak to the party, but telling her the story reminded me that I had promised my brothers I would only be gone for a short time. I looked at my brother's phone to see that not only was it already 1:45am, but Daveon had been blowing up the burner, sending me into panic mode.

"Aye, I need to go see what my brother calling for," I said.

"Okay," she said, "I'll see you later then."

I knew it was my moment. I didn't look around, or ask, or hesitate. Right then, I nearly knocked her nose off with mine when I slammed my face into hers to kiss her on the lips. When I stopped, her expression verified that I had stunned her, but a smile quickly followed, to my relief. I walked away smiling and looked up to see that my boys saw that whole thing. Their wide eyes and mouths displayed their shock, and they were smiling at me like I had won the party. I crowned myself king of the night and didn't have a care in the world until I remembered I needed to call my brother.

I stepped outside on the porch, with thoughts of the worst-case scenario swarming through my head. Kemis must have discovered I was gone, and was out in his truck, riding around the neighborhood looking for me. If someone was riding around looking for their kid, the house would have been easy to spot with the constant traffic going in and out, and people hanging outside on the porch and in the yard.

I called Daveon to see what was going on.

"Bro, where you at? You said you'd be back before one, and you ain't been answering. Jay over here losing it!" Daveon said in a hushed but angry tone.

"My bad, Day. I lost track of time talking to this girl. I'm outside; I'm coming home now," I said.

"Okay but look, K still downstairs with this girl talking. They were sitting out front for a little bit, but they came back in and sat in the front room. Just make sure they ain't outside when you walk up," he said.

"I got you. Good looking out. Make sure the window not locked and tell Jay I'm good."

I ended the call, nervous that getting back was going to be more challenging than getting out had been. Seeing that I had walked outside, Jon, Josh, and Terrel came outside to see what I was doing.

"You leaving?" Josh asked.

"Yeah man," I said. "I told my brothers I wouldn't be gone long, and Jason being extra. Ay where you get that chain from?" I asked Josh, admiring the shiny gold chain with a large cross pendant he displayed around his neck. He always had nice jewelry that he would emphasize to everyone was real and "not that fake shit."

"You roll with me, and I'll get you right. Then you stop looking rough, and Lakisha will getchu that invite back to her crib after the next party!" he said.

"Whatchu mean, nigga? She invited me today!"

They all laughed, knowing I was lying.

We said our goodbyes and parted ways, and I plotted how I would get back inside the apartment without incident. It was a short walk home, since Terron's house was only a few streets over from mine and about five blocks up. I didn't see Kemis or his date on the front steps when I drew close, but the downstairs lights were on, signaling they were likely still hanging out.

Despite my best attempts to climb the tree without making any noise, the sounds of the leaves rustling alerted a dog near another apartment building across the lot. It began announcing my presence, loudly barking and wildly running back and forth. Unsure if I should jump down and hide until the dog stopped barking or climb faster in case someone came outside to check on the dog, I decided faster was the way.

I scurried up to the branch nearest the roof, and attempted to lean over just enough to step one foot onto the rooftop, but I lost my footing and slipped, banging my knee on the edge of the rooftop. It was a small tumble, and I landed with my hands firmly placed on the rooftop, one foot planted in the tree, while the other dangled in the air.

While I was fortunate to not have toppled down to the ground below, my crash caused the dog to wildly race around and bark even louder, and the sounds of the barking and my minor crash caught the attention of Daveon, who appeared at his bedroom window. He quickly ducked out of sight as the front door opened, followed by Kemis' voice underneath me at the front door. I quickly raised my dangling leg onto the roof and crouched my head down, flattening my body on top of the portico roof with my arms closely tucked by my sides in hopes I wasn't discovered.

"Can't stand that daggone dog," Kemis said after he opened the front door and escorted out his guest. "Someone should report them people. They not even allowed to have a dog over here," he said. He walked his guest to her car and opened the door so she could get in. "I'm sorry. I didn't mean to keep you so late. I really enjoyed your company though."

"I enjoyed yours even more," she responded. "Your little brothers were so sweet to give you some privacy."

"Yeah, they can be cool when they wanna be. I better make sure they ain't up there getting into trouble."

I watched as the two of them embraced one another, and he planted a kiss on her mouth, similar to the one I had given Lakisha at the party, except his was much more graceful.

Kemis went back inside after she drove away, causing me uncertainty with how to proceed. Fortunately, Jason quietly opened the window and whispered for me to hurry. I quickly complied and crawled through the window and immediately heard Kemis walking up the steps.

"Dude, take off your clothes! Hurry up!" said Daveon, the expert when it came to sneaking back in. He had earlier instructed me to wear basketball shorts under my jeans. I stripped faster than I ever had while Jason closed the window and then flung my clothing into their closet. I flew onto Jason's bed and pretended to be engulfed in the television while Jason pretended to be casually scrolling through IG on his phone, right as Kemis walked in.

"I thought I heard something. Clay, I didn't know you were still up. What y'all watching?"

I briefly studied the television, realizing I had no idea how to respond to his question.

Fortunately, Jason chimed in with the save. "He been dozing off for most of the show! Just quit fighting and go to bed dude!"

"I know," I fake laughed, "I was trying to hang, but I'm 'bout to go to bed." I got up pretending to yawn and headed out to my room.

"I feel you. I've had a long night too so I'ma go ahead and turn in. Night y'all," Kemis said as he left.

"Night," we said in unison.

My heart raced, and I struggled to take quiet, slow breaths, not believing I had actually pulled off a midnight sneak-out. I waddled off to my room, pretending to be sleepy in case my brother was lingering near the hallway, and let out a huge sigh of relief after closing the door to our room. I was disappointed that Tay was already in a deep sleep, and I would have to wait until the next day to share with him all the details of my victorious night.

We sleepily piled one by one into our tiny kitchen the next morning and talked over bowls of cereal, while Kemis sat at the table groggily perusing his schoolwork. He filled us in on his night with his guest Kory, a girl he had met at church. She was a law school student and sang in the choir, and Kemis said they had previously talked a few times at church. I did recall seeing Kemis speak with her on a few occasions after church was over when the rest of us desperately wanted to leave.

Jason started talking about how late Kory had stayed over. "K, I can't be raising no nephews right now," he joked. Kemis had always told us that we better not bring him home any nephews when my brothers were about to go out with girls.

"Oh so you funny! It's definitely not like that. First of all, we're just friends. And secondly, we plan to honor God with our relationship, even if it does become more serious in the future.

So, there won't be any of that. We had really good conversation and just lost track of time," Kemis said.

He felt the need to explain that the two of them remained in the front room all night, just talking and watching shows. He told us he liked her, but that he didn't plan on pursuing something serious anytime soon. I wondered if it was because he was in charge of all of us, but I didn't want to ask him.

"Bro, but she fine fine. You telling me y'all didn't kiss or nothing the whole time she was here?" Jason asked, but his expression already said that he didn't believe it.

I almost let it slip that I saw them kissing in the parking lot but caught myself before it escaped out of my mouth.

Kemis laughed and said, "I gave her a kiss goodnight outside. But that's it, and that's all there will be. It's possible to just enjoy a girl's company, which is what I did. We talked and laughed and ate and made lattes. It's been a while since I hung out with a nice girl. It was pretty cool actually."

"Dang bro. I'm proud of you," Jason said as Kemis smiled. "You've officially become the lamest dude I know! She sat here all that time and didn't go to your room? And this nigga said lattes!"

Jason and Daveon cracked up laughing, and Tay and I smiled, while Kemis just rolled his eyes and shook his head.

"I'll make lattes if it'll keep me from making nephews, bro," Kemis said.

4

LITTLE FUN, BIG TROUBLE

While everyone was normally talking about a social media post, the latest episode of a popular show, or the most recent fight, at school that Monday, all everyone was talking about was the party from Friday night and the people that attended. I swelled with pride thinking my popularity points had increased as word spread that I was there kissing one of the prettiest girls at school.

My boys filled me in on things I missed before I arrived at the party and after I left. There were all sorts of rumors about who was kissing who, and who took someone else's girlfriend to the backroom of the house. There was a story about one kid who had stumbled home drunk, and their mom walked over to the party to find out what was going on. Around that time a fight had broken out in the front yard, prompting the end of the party since a neighbor yelled and said they were calling the police.

A different kid from our school arrived home high after smoking, and his mother took him to the emergency room because of how he was behaving. He smoked some "bad weed," as it was called, that may have been laced with something else.

She called the police, who contacted the school. The principal, after getting word of the party, started calling parents of kids he was told were at the party in hopes that an informant would snitch on whoever distributed the weed. Josh had already been called into the principal's office and was filling us in on the details.

While I had convinced myself over the weekend that sneaking out was easy, in that moment I didn't feel equipped for the type of suspense and anxiety associated with keeping an outing that risky from my oldest brother.

"Yo," I told them, "make sure y'all keep my name out yo' mouth if he asks y'all something."

"I know you ain't worried since you running thangs at the crib!" Josh replied snarkily. We all laughed. They knew I wasn't running anything, and I knew too, but I still felt obligated to pretend so I could act as though I had the same freedoms they enjoyed.

When school let out, Lakisha told me she had a good time hanging with me at the party, and it temporarily made me forget about the principal's inquiries. But then she told me that her name was on a list of kids at the party, and that her mom got called, and she found herself in the principal's officer during fourth period. She reassured me that she repeatedly denied being there, even though the principal did not seem to believe her.

We got home to find Kemis, Jay, and Daveon outside talking near the porch with one of the neighbors from down the street. It was an unusually warm and sunny fall day, and a lot of people were outside on their porches and in the parking lot taking advantage of the weather.

"Can I go to the court after my homework?" I asked Kemis after our greetings were over.

He frowned at me. "You know you still on punishment."

I had hoped he would chill for the day since it was so nice out, but that wasn't happening. Even though I yearned to be down the street, I knew it was probably best since I only had three days until my next science quiz, and I had made plans to study every day so I could get my phone back. I joined Tay in our room to get started on my homework and to study for my quiz.

Our bedroom window was propped open, allowing us to hear even more clearly the joyous sounds of people outside playing in the water from the fire hydrant that had been busted open by some neighborhood kids. Other kids were out playing and talking, while my brothers were out chatting it up with their friends. Everything was peaceful, but it was the calm before the storm.

"Clay, I got this strange call from Mr. Mack," Kemis said.

He had come into the room after Tay and I had been quietly doing homework for a few minutes.

My mouth and stomach immediately grew sick while I silently waited for his next sentence. There had been many calls from Mr. Mack to Kemis, formerly to Granny before she passed, and they usually weren't with any good news. I was certain that Kemis' phone was saved into Mr. Mack's favorites list, for the convenience of one-button dialing. On one occasion, he did call to say my teachers told him that my behavior had improved, but that was short-lived. Usually, he called to talk to my brother about my worsening behavior.

Between Daveon a couple of years before and myself, Mr. Mack had spoken to Granny and then Kemis likely hundreds of times. He had regular complaints about the two of us, while he absolutely loved Tay. Tay represented the school in the regional spelling bee, a math competition, a coding competition that he had won, and a chess competition. When Mr. Mack saw us at school together, he always called us two of his favorites, but I knew he was really only talking about Tay.

Kemis went on. "He told me he got word you were at some party on Friday night where some kid smoked weed and got sick.

He said he spoke to at least three different students who said you were at this party after midnight. But I told him there was absolutely no way. I told him I saw with my own eyes that you dozed off since you weren't allowed to play video games, then watched a movie with your brothers, and then went to bed.

"Someone must've just dropped your name since your friends Josh and Terrell, and that other one was there. I told you before I don't think them boys are any good. You don't want to listen to me, but look at them now, at this party smoking weed again. They mamas don't never know where they at! And Mr. Mack said this kid had all kinds of stuff in his system! Not just weed. Just crazy," he said.

"Yeah, pretty crazy," I said, nervously hoping the conversation was permanently over.

I glanced over at Tay while Kemis walked out. He had a slight look of relief that he seemed to be trying to mask by intensely staring at his laptop. He looked like he couldn't handle any more close calls, and I knew I couldn't either.

I was looking down at my books when Kemis' phone dinged in the hallway, quickly followed by a second ding. Relieved that he was no longer discussing the party, I refused to look up at him, and was trying to keep a straight face and pretend like I was still doing what I was supposed to. I knew I had to look calm and unworried, so I fixed my gaze on my homework and tried my best to look like I was being responsible and dutifully studying for my upcoming quiz.

Kemis pounced over and closed the top drawer to my dresser. At least, that's what I thought I had heard. In hindsight, I realized he was pulling a belt out the drawer, and I wished I had realized it sooner. I hadn't even seen him advance towards me when he asked his next question. "What's this?"

I glanced up to see a picture on his phone that showed a bunch of kids having a good time—including me and Lakisha—at

Terron's party. A red arrow had been added to the picture, that pointed to the top of my head. After looking at it I immediately regretted having on basketball shorts, as he quickly yanked me up and used the belt to lash and thrash my backside with the strength of Batman.

I shrieked so loudly that Daveon ran into the room to make sure I was okay, but then quickly turned around once he witnessed what was happening. "K, bro, chill!" I pleaded in between painful strikes.

I tried to block to no avail, and quickly jumped over to the bed, crab-legged onto the floor and out of his reach until I surged into the hallway and down the steps while he yelled for me to return. Refusing to voluntarily return to a beatdown, I stooped to pick up a pair of Tay's shoes near the front door and fled barefoot out of the door and down the sidewalk towards the basketball court.

I kept looking back for the first twenty seconds or so, and then stopped to slide my feet into the shoes once I convinced myself I was no longer being chased. My sprint was restarted once the shoes were laced, and I ran all the way until I had arrived safely at the basketball court.

Josh and Terrell were already there, and I joined in a game that was already underway. I was mad I couldn't run home and get my normal basketball shoes, but I knew I had to work with what I had.

"You ever get called to the principal?" Josh asked in between games.

"Naw, but he sent my brother a picture of me at the party. Somebody out here snitching!" I said.

"Bruh, that's crazy. Whoever did that—they lame as hell," he said.

After a while, one of the older guys at the basketball court called my brothers' names, and Jason and Daveon were walking towards us.

"Y'all coming in?" someone asked. Everyone loved when Jason, the best baller in the area, stayed to play so they could challenge him on the court.

"Naw, bruh. Just gotta get my brother," Jason said.

I rolled my eyes realizing that they had come to drag me home to face Kemis.

"Baby bro, remember that promise you made us that you ain't getting caught?" Jason asked as he approached me.

"It wasn't my fault, Jay. Some lame ass sent a picture!" I said.

"Then it is yo' fault, 'cause your lame ass shouldn't have been dumb enough to be on camera. Come on, we gotta walk you home since my keys just got took," said Jason.

I told my boys I had to go as I trailed down the sidewalk behind my brothers, who cracked jokes on me the entire walk for the way I screamed and yelled when Kemis hit me earlier. They told me that after I left, Kemis got Tay next since he had lied to him the night I snuck out, and then went after Daveon, who sprinted out the back door and went to hang with a neighbor until Kemis calmed down.

"I'm just glad I wasn't there," Jason said with a laugh. "K crazy sometimes. Clay, you got the whole house in trouble, and you know Unc coming later."

Kemis called for us to come eat after the three of us returned inside. Almost every week, one of the ladies from the church prepared meals for us and brought them by on Sundays after church, something they had been doing since Granny passed away. The food usually lasted us at least three or four nights each week, and tasted better than what my older brothers cooked.

Dinner started off unusually quiet, other than the commentary on how delicious the food was. While I thought about apologizing for sneaking out, I was too mad at Kemis for hitting me, and I was too embarrassed about getting my brothers in trouble to engage in my normal chatter.

While the four of us were quiet, I knew Kemis was too upset to remain quiet all night. He began speaking to us while his gaze remained fixed on his plate.

"So, we had an interesting afternoon. Or maybe I should say, I had an interesting afternoon, since I was the last one to be let in on a little secret everyone else in this house knew about but me," Kemis said.

His voice was still angry, but quieter than when he was yelling at me to come back to my room earlier. I was compelled to say something in defense of my brothers. "K, it ain't they fault—"

"Clay, be quiet. I'm talking right now," he said.

"But I was the one that did it!" I was trying not to yell, but I needed him to understand how bad I felt for getting everyone in trouble. "And they ain't—"

"I said BE QUIET!"

"Damn, you ain't gotta yell all the fucking time!" I said as I got up to get more water.

I approached the sink and groaned from feeling the strike of his shoe on my back between my shoulders, and he continued talking as though he hadn't hurled a shoe over the table to strike me.

"Jason, you seventeen, and when one of your brothers, especially one that's only twelve, asks you to help him do something he shouldn't do, the responsible thing to do is to tell him no. You have a job, a car, and responsibilities, and one of those responsibilities is to help keep your brothers *out* of trouble, not to help them get into it. You helped him sneak to a party where kids are drinking, getting high, fighting, and who knows what other kind of madness. I mean, I wouldn't expect you to help any of them do that, but definitely not your baby brother," he said.

"I'm not no baby though, and it ain't like we ain't all smoked before," I said.

"Clay, I swear if you say one more thing, I might kick you in the throat!" he said.

I was irritated with his threat, but fell silent knowing Kemis' patience was getting thinner by the second.

"Jay, I'ma hold yo' keys for a week. Clay, I already got your phone, and now I don't know when you're getting it back. Day and Tay, I might be taking yours too! Y'all straight up running around here lying to me so he can act crazy, knowing he already been bad as hell lately," he said.

We heard the front door open and slam shut, and the sounds of Ma stumbling up the steps into her room.

Kemis turned to me. "Clay, take Ma some water."

I unwillingly left my seat to do what I was told. It was a job I hated but was usually the one designated to do it. On the rare nights that she actually came home, she needed water for her medications that we all knew she wasn't taking.

She never spoke and told us to come in when it was time for water, so I cracked open the door once I reached the top of the steps.

"Hey, Clay," she muttered in a whisper without making any eye contact. She sat lifelessly on her bed and stared blankly at the muted television. She hardly ever spoke unless it was to ask if there was food left.

"Hey Ma, I got your water," I said.

I tiptoed over items on the floor to reach the table next to her bed, where I moved some stuff aside to find a spot for the glass. I could tell she had moved a bunch of stuff over to the other side of her bed so that she had enough room to prop her feet. I had never seen her room, or even her bed, completely cleaned. The partially covered mattress was usually overflowing with clothes, mail, magazines, spoons, lighters, toiletries, whatever she needed throughout the day or week. There was barely a path to get from the door to her table, and I stepped around her piles of things on the floor to make my way back out of the room.

I left out and closed the door without a word, knowing that if someone had asked her what color my shirt was, she probably couldn't have answered.

Ma didn't start living with us until Granny had passed away, and even after that she stayed for about a week and then left for another month before beginning a series of sporadic returns. When she would leave for lengthy periods, Kemis would clean her room out and sleep in there instead of the basement.

We had no idea where she had been staying before Granny's death. Uncle Vel, one of our uncles who was in prison, would say Ma was "in the streets" or hopping from house to house, or on drugs, depending on what guy she was with. Kemis didn't like her living with us, but often shared that he felt too guilty to kick her out.

The kitchen had largely been deserted when I arrived back downstairs, other than Kemis, who stood at the counter preparing a plate for Ma.

"You're on kitchen duty this week," he said as he fist-bumped me on my arm, adding insult to injury.

I moped over to dig the rag out of the sink and started with cleaning the table and the counters. I was sweeping the floor when Jason came and took the broom out of my hands. I figured he was taking it away to knock my face in for getting him in trouble. Instead, he looked at me and started sweeping.

"I got kitchen duty," I sorrowfully reminded him.

"Go ahead and start the dishes man. I got you," he said as he continued sweeping. When he finished, he stood next to me and started helping with the dishes.

"I ain't mean to get yo' keys took," I said, but he put up his hand, motioning me to stop.

"Bro, you've covered for me a hundred times," he said. "But at the end of the day, K right. I shoulda looked out for you, and I didn't."

"Whatchu about to be lame now?" I asked.

"I ain't never been lame lil' dude," he said as he pushed me. "I am your big brother, you know—I'm *supposed* to watch out for you."

I didn't really know what he meant; I thought he had always been a good brother. He never seemed bothered when I asked to tag along with him to places. He would bring me to basketball practice with him on the weekends, and we would talk about the plays and his teammates and how he did. On occasion, the coach would let me join in the scrimmage. Many times, we would stay late after practice, and Jason would shoot around with me—those were some of my most fun Saturdays, especially when I got to scrimmage with Jason and his teammates.

Sometimes he would let me ride with him to his friends' houses if I wasn't on punishment. And sometimes, even when I was on punishment, he would let me hang out in his room late, after Kemis was asleep, and let me use his iPad or play video games with him. But I still felt like they were always treating me like I was a little kid, which I hated. The night of the party was the first time I felt like they had treated me like one of them.

"K got in yo' little bad ass, didn't he," he teased.

I frowned but always had a comeback. "Same way he got in yours when you smashed that girl raw in your room," I said, knowing I had him.

"Oooohhh you got the clapback again, huh! You don't even know what that means!" he said, but I had sat in on enough of their talks about girls and heard their stories.

My clapback didn't stop him from teasing me about getting caught, which I wasn't exactly ready to laugh about yet. I kept wondering if I had left that party when I said I would, could it have prevented me from being caught on anyone's stupid cell phone video. I felt horrible for not keeping my word and leaving when I told my brothers that I would. I knew I wouldn't convince them to let me sneak out to anything for a long time.

5

LECTURED

I was isolated in my room later on since Tay was in the room with Jason and Daveon when Pastor D came into the house and greeted Kemis.

Pastor D was one of the only adults in my life that I actually liked, and I had known him for as far back as I could remember. He had been in our lives so long that we called him "Unc." Although we weren't blood related to him, he had always made us feel like we were. Granny had joined our church when I was little, and Pastor D had been Kemis' youth pastor when he was in middle and high school. He was someone we saw regularly outside of church, other than Granny's prayer group friends.

I didn't enjoy our forced attendance to church or to the youth group, and had learned long ago how to tune out the Bible stories and boring sermons while I made up stories in my head or tried to talk to some of the girls in attendance like my older brothers often did. There were times when we were supposed to be in youth church, and Daveon and I would sneak off to hang around outside or find some girls to talk to, but Pastor D would leave out to come find us and make us go back inside. The girls and the threat of Kemis keeping our phones was what kept us going back regularly.

Pastor D was a regular visitor at our apartment and was always checking on us to make sure we had food, school supplies, socks, clothes, or anything we needed. There were times when we had power outages, and he always showed up to make sure we were okay, even if it was still storming outside. If Kemis didn't have money to send us on a field trip at school or money for one of us to play sports, Pastor D always helped where he could. But what I liked most about him was that he was one of the few people that Kemis would listen to, and my older brothers often called him if they wanted him to come over and talk sense into Kemis.

Sometimes Kemis would drop us off at his house, or we would all go over there together just to hang out or have a big dinner. When Kemis and Jason were having some rough patches, we were over there a lot. I liked being there because there was a basketball hoop in the backyard, and Pastor D's son Caleb would beg us to play with him on his video games.

While alone I thought about Pastor D, who was married to a beautiful lady, Sister Robin, who we called "Auntie," and their two kids, Caleb and Sophie, who were younger than us. I presumed they never had issues with money, as they lived in one of those quiet neighborhoods on a street with only a few houses that hardly anyone ever entered.

I wondered if his kids thought he was the perfect dad, who always talked to them about all of their problems. I knew firsthand that their mother cooked the most delicious meals, and I figured she did their laundry and folded it inside their house without going to a laundromat down the street, and helped them with their homework every day.

I wondered what it was like to live a perfect suburban life where they could order pizza and sit at the door and wait for a large, warm pizza to show up. Kemis said the pizza man used to come to our neighborhood a lot. I knew, because I was only six years old when I watched the guys next door rob the pizza man. They gave me a slice of pizza and five dollars to keep quiet about it. When the police came around asking questions, the officers suspected Jason and Daveon of the crime, but Granny wouldn't let them question any of us.

Days later I asked the guys if I could be their lookout for some more exploits, but they told me I would have to wait until I was ten. By that time, they were all gone. One moved with his auntie to Texas. The other was gunned down around the corner, nearly one year after the pizza robbery. The last one was in prison for trying to rob the mailman.

"Clay? You in there?" Pastor D inquired while tapping on the door.

"Yeah, you can come in," I said.

Pastor D strolled in with a faint smile on his face and a curious look in his eyes.

"I think you know what I want to talk to you about," he told me as he took a seat next to me on my bed. I felt like he would be biased in his discussion since he had already spoken to Kemis first. I instantly felt guilty and a little defensive. Since the last time he had come over, I had been in a lot of trouble, and I anticipated that he was going to ask some hard questions. "Your brother gave me his version of how school is going."

I looked at the ground and played with my thumbs, anything to avoid his eyes. His eyes were always bright and his voice soft. He had a laid-back demeanor most of the time, with a few exceptions, like the occasional time when he preached during Sunday service and his voice would get a little louder.

He continued on calmly, "I think I normally ask about you and your friends and what y'all have been getting into, but Kemis filled me in on some of that too. But I don't want to come in here with any preconceived notions. So, why don't you tell me in your own words what's going on with you that's causing you to get into so much trouble. Between the incident where you cheated on your test and cussed out your teacher, and now sneaking out with your friends, it kinda seems like your behavior is getting worse and not better."

I hadn't considered whether my behavior was worsening. Normally I was just mouthing off a little bit at school and sometimes at home. I often snuck out to the basketball court when I wasn't supposed to, and sometimes stayed there past the time I had been told to be home. From time to time, I had been skipping class, and occasionally skipping school altogether to hang out with my boys. I had been in a fight or two, and then there was that time I was caught in the girl's bathroom stall with a girl. I guessed cheating on tests and sneaking out of the house were sort of new.

I wanted him to pose basic yes or no questions; I wasn't interested in offering an explanation of all my thoughts and feelings. There were a million things I could've said, and a thousand things I wanted to say, but I just wasn't sure how to say it, and offered only a shoulder shrug in response to his inquiry.

"Kemis and I just prayed for you, Clay. He prays for you often, and so do I. I pray that you find godly friends and influences. Today we prayed that the Lord order your steps and direct your way, that He leads you in the right paths, and that you follow Him. When you were at that party on Friday night, did you feel like you were supposed to be there?" he asked.

"I don't know. My boys were gon' be there. And then I got there and saw Lakisha, and I got to talk to her more than we talk at school. I ain't even do anything bad and I still got in trouble," I said.

"Are you telling me you snuck out in the middle of the night just to see a girl you can see at school? And you don't think that's pretty bad?"

"It ain't like that, Unc! I was just hanging out wit' my boys, but she was there too!"

"When I was younger at those house parties, some kids would go into back rooms and do all kinds of stuff!" he said.

I couldn't imagine Pastor D at a house party. The thought was funny, even though I knew he spoke accurately. There were a lot of kids sneaking off at Terron's party, which I learned from my boys earlier that morning, but I stayed out in the open with Lakisha. I wished I hadn't, since maybe sneaking off to the back would have prevented me from being filmed.

I was honest with my reply. "All we did was kiss, and we weren't in no room or nothing. We just talked and kissed, and then I left after that anyway. I didn't even smoke weed this time or drink. K mad at me for being at one party and kissing when he knows he's done way more than that."

He kept going, "For one, he's an adult, and much older than you. Secondly, I think you know better than to think he's upset just because you were at a party. You know how some of these parties go—we hear it on the news all the time, a fight breaks out and someone starts shooting, and next thing you know a bunch of people are hurt or worse. Your actions have an impact on more than just you. What if the police broke up the party and had taken you and called DFS or hotlined your brother?" he asked.

When Granny died, Pastor D was the one that asked an attorney at church to help Kemis file a petition to be our legal guardian. It seemed like a long process, and a social worker had to come to the house and talk to us and monitor us before it was all over. Pastor D knew there could be serious repercussions if they thought somehow that Kemis wasn't capable of taking care of us, and a call to DFS because of me could have meant the separation of me and my brothers.

It was always one of the biggest fears in our house—that we would get a hotline call, and some judge would decide my brother wasn't fit enough to raise us, and the system would separate us and try to make us live with crazy people. But we had already designated a spot in the city where we would meet should we all get ripped apart and have to break out of foster homes. We had resolved that no judge would keep us apart, even if it meant we would reside in a vacant building until we could either convince our auntie from out of state to get us or until I turned eighteen.

"Unc, nothing like that happened—I just went in, hollered at my boys, hollered at old girl, just like normal stuff everybody does."

"Everybody does that? At one in the morning?" he asked.

"The party actually started at like nine. I only went out after midnight because I had to make sure K thought—"

"Thought you were asleep so you could sneak out of the house and go somewhere you knew you weren't supposed to be," Pastor D interrupted.

I knew that Pastor D, being over twenty years older than Kemis, would definitely not understand why I had done what I had done when Kemis didn't even understand. He had kids of his own, and generally treated us like his kids, and most of the things he told us only reinforced the things Kemis said.

"This all I'm saying—if the party had been at seven o'clock that night, or even four o'clock that day, K still would've said no. It ain't matter what time, so the only way I was getting there was by sneaking out!"

"Clay, first of all, weren't you still on punishment for the school incident?" he asked.

I sighed.

"Okay, secondly, you snuck out to hang with the same friends that you've been getting in trouble with since kindergarten?" he asked.

I rolled my eyes at him. "I do more with them than just get in trouble. We hoop, play spades, watch YouTube and play video games. We do all kinds of normal stuff! But since he made up his mind about them already, if I say their name, he don't want me out—which ain't cool cause those are my only friends. He, well he and you, judge them all for a couple of things that happened forever ago," I said.

I had known Jon, Terrell, and Josh since the second grade, when the four of us were all in the same class for the first time. We didn't realize it at the time, but it later became clear that the school made sure the four of us were never assigned to the same classroom together for the remainder of elementary school. The four of us would come up with the craziest, dumbest ideas, from throwing classroom supplies out the doors and windows, gluing items together that didn't belong together, running into the hallways to yell random phrases out loud, and putting water on crumples of paper and throwing them at the ceiling to watch them temporarily stick. My favorite times were when we would run into occupied girls' bathrooms and turn out all the lights before quickly running out.

Granny whooped me nearly every day in the second grade, since that was how often the teacher contacted her. At first, my teacher would send notes home with Tay, but when Tay and I caught on, we would throw the notes out the window on the school bus. Daveon warned us that Granny would find out, which she did after a few weeks, and whooped Tay and me for throwing out the notes.

After that, the teacher switched from notes to phone calls. I tried to stop those too. When we could see on the caller ID that the number was from the school, my brothers would help me intercept the call, since Granny hardly ever beat us to the phone. Jason would pick up the phone and pretend to be my uncle since his voice was a little deeper at the time. One time, Daveon told my teacher to call back at midnight, and she did. I found out because Granny came in and whooped me ten minutes after midnight, as I remembered seeing the time on the digital clock in our room.

Then Josh convinced me to break the teacher's phone, thinking that would keep her from calling. The caper that consisted of me dropping her cell phone in the toilet in the boys' bathroom did not end well since I almost lost my life when the principal told Granny she would have to pay for my teacher's phone. Granny fell on the front stoop when chasing after me with a metal spatula raised over her head, which I was convinced made her hit me even harder when she did catch me later that night.

The first time my entire crew got suspended all together was in the fifth grade. I got into a fight with a kid whose boys jumped in, causing my squad to jump in too. In the sixth grade, Josh brought weed to school, and the four of us skipped class to go smoke it. Principal Mack caught us and threatened to have us expelled if we didn't say who brought the weed. None of us would snitch, so we all ended up getting a five-day suspension.

"Clay, you have gotten into a lot of trouble with these guys, so the people that love you are going to feel some type of way about them. I would never call them bad kids, because for all I know that's what their families are saying about you. But it definitely seems like they are not benefitting you. If you had snuck out to study for a math test or snuck out to celebrate that Josh got all A's on his report card, maybe I'd have a different opinion. But you snuck out to be somewhere you had no business being.

"I know it's tempting to do what your friends are doing, but what our friends are doing is not always the will of God. Let me ask you something: do you think I would let Caleb play in the street just because he wanted to?"

I shook my head.

"Of course not," he said. "Because I love him, and I'm in charge of protecting him. When Caleb was real little, he thought it was funny to run towards the street because he knew I would chase him. He didn't listen to me when I told him to stop, and I was terrified he would keep it up and get hit by a car! One day I popped him for not listening and running towards the street, and he was so mad at me. He laughs at it now, knowing that he was crazy for wanting to run into the street. But when he was real small, he was too young to comprehend the danger of his actions.

"I know you've seen more in your young life than a lot of kids your age. But there are many people wiser than you, that still know more than you about life. Your brother is one of those people. He only wants what's good for you. Your job is to obey him if you want to be right in the eyes of the Lord," he continued.

I hated when people talked about obeying, and I longed for the conversation to be over, even with knowing that the only thing I would be allowed to do that night was homework. I liked Pastor D better when we were just hanging out and watching basketball.

"Not all older brothers could handle what yours has taken on. When I was twenty-two, I definitely wasn't mature enough to raise a child, and he's raising four very special young men. He deserves your respect *and* your obedience. And that also means you need to stop using profanity towards him like I heard you been doing, young man," he said.

"Well look," he changed the subject and reached in his wallet and pulled out a ten-dollar bill. Pastor D was always giving us something, whether it was food, desserts, games, or money. "Pick yourself something up at McDonald's this week. I wasn't going to give you this when your brother told me you were acting up. I was gonna give you this instead," he said as he balled up his fist and smiled.

I smiled back before I put the money in my pocket.

"But Clay, the Lord doesn't withhold his good things from us, even when we fall short, so who am I to withhold mine. I plan to see you soon, and I hope by then you're making wiser choices," he said.

Before I could respond he grabbed my hand and started praying, and I wasn't sure how to respond. At first, I bowed my head, and then closed my eyes, but then tears welled up in my eyes, and I wasn't sure why. I knew I had behaved badly, yet I felt this weird sense of love and peace, coupled with an overwhelming feeling that I needed to change and do better.

I could tell by the things he prayed that he had really listened to the things I had said. He prayed about my choices, my friends, and even said their names. He prayed for my grades, my teachers, my brothers, and even Lakisha. I was intrigued by how he talked to God like he actually knew God, and like God knew me, and I wondered why he was so confident that God would hear the concerns of a kid who had not done anything good in a long time.

"I want you and Tay to come over for dinner Friday night. Is that cool?" he asked after standing to head out of the room.

I nodded in response, since I usually enjoyed being at his house—unless I was there because I was suspended from school.

"Alright, I love you. Stay yo' butt out of trouble, you hear me?" he asked.

I nodded again.

"No no, I want an answer from your mouth," he said.

"I will," I said, and I meant it, knowing I needed to stay clear of the trouble scene for a while.

Pastor D talked and prayed individually with all my brothers before he left, something he regularly did with us. Afterwards, Kemis walked him to his car while I watched them both from the front door as they stood outside talking for a few more minutes, followed by an embrace. I had always wondered what made Pastor D want to spend so much time with us, especially since we really had nothing to offer him for the time and help that he had given to us.

I wanted desperately to go to bed after he left, but I didn't need Kemis on my case about not finishing my homework. I had been working for about fifteen minutes when Tay came back into the bedroom.

"You alright," he asked as he sat on his bed and broke his silence.

"I'm cool. You mad at me?" I asked.

"Naw bro, I'm cool."

I enviously watched as he put on his headphones and reclined back to play on his phone. I wondered if I was even capable of staying out of trouble the way Tay did. While he wasn't perfect, he almost always behaved as though our brother was around, with only a few exceptions. Sometimes he would doze off in church and Granny or Kemis would thump him. I once saw him throw food in a food fight at school. He tongue-kissed a girl at the library once and kept asking Kemis to drop him off at the library so he could see her and have secret rendezvous in the quiet section of the stacks. A couple of times he snuck onto his game system after Kemis told us to go to bed. I knew he had helped some of his friends at school by giving them answers on tests. But those instances were few and far between. I could never understand how he seemed to be so good without a lot of effort.

One thing was clear—he was much smarter than me. He had warned me that my sneak-out was a bad idea, and I wasn't sure if my punishment this time was worth the few minutes of fun I had, especially since the best part of the night was talking to a girl that I probably could've talked to on the phone if I hadn't been on punishment. Plus, my brothers had gotten into trouble for helping me. After thinking about it, I concluded the sneak-out hadn't been worth the trouble, but those sentiments would soon change.

6

OUT FOR BLOOD

"Bruh, what are these?" Terron asked as I rounded the corner in the locker room to find a group of my physical education classmates huddled around my locker while he held up my shoes. The others were pointing and laughing and entertaining themselves at my expense.

"Nigga them shoes trash! I ain't even know the dolla sto' sold shoes, bruh!" a kid named Ryan shouted and laughed, prompting laughter from the other boys in our row of lockers.

"Put my shit down, dude!" I snatched my shoes from Terron and rammed him into the locker, prompting him to rush toward me until he squared up with his face directly in front of mine.

"Ay fellas, break it up! If y'all spent as much energy into getting dressed as you did messing around you'd be out the locker room by now!" Coach Adams yelled. He didn't seem to understand that I wanted more than anyone to get dressed and get out of the locker room, away from the place where I could count on getting teased about something nearly every day I was there.

It had been a tortuous ending to yet another gym class where I came out of the shower and found my peers digging through my clothing for the sole purpose of finding something to laugh about.

It wasn't nearly as bad as the time they put a pair of underwear that had holes in them on display, and then tossed them up so high they got caught on top of the pipes that ran across the ceiling. Of course, they pointed and laughed any time they saw me the rest of that day since they knew I didn't have underwear on.

Being in the locker room after gym class was just one of the many activities at school that made me feel self-conscious, similar to the daily routine of standing in line with all the other kids who received free lunch. I hated that "free lunch kids" had a separate line to stand in than those who paid. Although it was probably more than half of the kids at school, it still felt like a badge of poverty that I was shamefully forced to display each day before joining my crew at our table.

I joined my friends at lunch that day after standing in the line of shame and listened to the rumors they shared about who leaked the video that led to my demise. They told me they had convinced Lakisha and some other girls to meet us at the basketball court after school. I doubted I would be able to join but pretended to be excited about it.

My chances of meeting my friends grew even slimmer after lunch. My math teacher called me to the board to complete a math problem, which I hated. Standing at the board in front of class felt even more shameful than standing in the free lunch line. I had long felt like she only called on the kids who she knew would get the answers wrong or the kids like me who never paid attention. It felt humiliating enough standing in front of everyone showing why X equaled 5, but to make matters worse, BJ, a kid who regularly cracked on my clothing, decided to show out again.

"Dang, bruh, did *all* yo' brothers wear that shirt before you wore it today?" he joked out loud, prompting snickering throughout the room. I looked down, still facing forward, and stared at my basic black t-shirt that I wore. It was a hand-me-down that likely originated with Daveon, and was slightly faded, but wasn't in tatters as BJ seemed to suggest. I thought about what Kemis told me, but it didn't take away the rage that was growing inside of my chest. Between the teasing from gym classmates, and now being subjected to taunting from BJ, I was willing and ready to be kicked out of school.

"Shut up, dude!" I said.

"Black ass nigga" BJ said. "They shoulda called yo' ass mud instead a Clay!" he added, causing the room to erupt in laughter.

"The fuck you say?" I asked.

"Clay, that's a write-up!" Mrs. Sebring said.

"Okay, so you'll write me up for saying some bullshit, but he allowed to talk about me and my shirt?" I asked.

She sat down at her desk and started typing on her computer as if she didn't hear me, while BJ, who remained comfortably smirking in the front row, started snickering with his friend. I stood back wanting to hit something, and decided that the something would be BJ's face. I walked up to him and socked him right in the middle of it, in hopes to sprain his sinus tract and render him unable to smell for life. I followed the first with a second hit that was so hard that his entire desk and chair fell back with him still seated in it, and I caught myself on my tiptoes to keep from falling over on top of it. He rolled over onto his side once he hit the floor, groaning and holding his nose.

His friend Damien, who was seated next to him, stood up and pushed me after seeing BJ on the floor, and I pushed him back and quickly followed the push with successive punches to his face. He had on a crisp, white Nike brand t-shirt that looked as though it had never been worn, and I was gratified in seeing drops of blood sprinkle down the bright white fabric and onto the floor when he doubled over in pain.

By then, Mrs. Sebring was paging security through her walkie talkie while my classmates either oohed and scrambled to get away or pulled out their phones in anticipation of more recordable events. I calmly grabbed my backpack amidst a sea of snares and quiet commentary from my other classmates, knowing I would be escorted out, and paced toward the hallway to await my escort.

Mr. Jones, the security guard, arrived and verified with my teacher that I was the one who needed to go.

"Young man, you at it again huh? One of these days they gon' kick you out for good!" he warned as we traversed the halls with his hand on my shoulder.

"Good. I hate it here," I said as we reached the long stretch of hallway towards the principal's office.

I blankly stared at the principal's mouth as he parted his lips to lecture me and tell me I was suspended for another five days.

"Clay, you've had fights before, but I've never seen you just attack someone. You want to tell me what made you decide to hit these boys?" Principal Mack asked.

I shook my head while I stared off at the wall, wondering if he was miserable with having to face boring brown walls all day with pastel-colored paintings that were probably as old as the school building. We sat in silence other than the commands I shouted at myself inside my brain to tell him the truth, but I didn't want to bring more attention to my shirt by telling him what happened, and I had already pulled a jacket out of my backpack to cover up. I shuffled around in my seat while he continued to discuss my bad behavior, which he did until Kemis joined us in the office.

"So Kemis, this type of outburst is unacceptable, but also uncharacteristic. He was documented using profanity yet again. His teacher noted that one of the boys he punched said something about his shirt, but he's not interested in discussing it with me. I have no choice but to suspend him for this. I'm worried that we're going to eventually have to transition him to one of the alternative schools. Academically I don't think he needs to be there, but these boys' mothers are going to be going crazy when I call them to tell them what happened to their sons at school today," said Principal Mack.

"I understand, Mr. Mack." Kemis turned and looked at me. "Clay, what's up? You know you can't just hit people. What happened?"

I became more and more upset with each minute that I had sat in the office, allowing time for my ferocious anger to settle into sadness. His question caused my emotions to intensify, and the last thing I wanted was to cry in front of them, which was about to happen. I lowered my head even more and shrugged my shoulders.

"Well look, please feel free to reach out to discuss it further, or if you wish to appeal, okay? You have my cell phone so use it anytime Kemis," Principal Mack told him.

"Thank you, sir. Will do," Kemis said as he stood up. "Does he have any work he can take?"

"I will make sure to have it sent home with Tay," he said.

"I appreciate that. Come on, Clay, let's roll," Kemis said. He was on his phone texting as we walked out, and I knew he was probably texting Pastor D. "Why aren't you talking to me?" he asked after we took our seats in his truck.

I shook my head and offered a one-shoulder shrug, knowing he would think it was stupid to get into a fight over my shirt.

"Baby bro, you know how I feel about y'all starting fights. I have trained y'all to the point where you could cause some serious injuries or worse! You can't just go around hitting people for no reason," he said.

He ended up driving off without an answer from me and sent me to my room when we got home. I went upstairs waiting for him to come, but the first to come through the door nearly an hour later was Jason. The creaking from the floor and the door flying open prompted me to look up and watch as he climbed next to me on the bed. His lengthy frame lay prostrate on my bed, pulling my pillow underneath his chest and looking up at me with curiosity in his expression.

"Just tell me what's wrong so K don't come up here and whoop yo' ass. Why you hitting people at school?" he asked me.

I looked at him not wanting to answer, before averting my eyes.

"Bro, you tell me like everything. Wassup?" he asked.

"It's not gon' matter because at the end of the day I'm the only one in trouble. The teacher don't like me. The principal think all I do is get in trouble, and so does K. They not gon' listen to me!" I said.

"But you know I will, so why you actin' like that?" he asked.

I reluctantly told him what happened and included some background. "This dude talks about my shirts, my pants, my shoes, my color, my hair, and even my teeth like every day. The teachers hear him do it and don't say shit, probably 'cause they just think I get in trouble all the time, and they don't like me in their classes anyway. So she ain't say one word to him when he going in on my shirt in front of the whole class! But then I say a cuss word and she hears it loud and fucking clear and writes me up! He was cussin too and she ain't say nothing! I hate her. I hate that whole school!"

"You don't have to cancel the whole school though," he told me.

"Fuck them! They all just label me…as broke, dark, nappy headed, with messed up teeth and clothes. And the teachers just think I'm bad, and they say I should be in special school," I said.

While there was normally no subject that was off limits with Jason, this topic was particularly hard. His school experience had always been different from mine, and I doubted he could relate to what I shared. He was a tall, attractive athlete that all of the girls wanted to date, and all of the guys wanted to be associated with, especially after he became one of the top basketball recruits in the entire country.

His teachers seemed to cater to his every whim—they'd offer extensions on his homework and other assignments and let him make up tests if he told them he didn't feel ready, or if he earned a bad grade. If he had a slip-up of his tongue, they would assume another student egged him on, and never that he was the aggressor.

Not only that, but Jason also had soft hair that waved up with hardly any effort, and almond brown skin that was smooth enough to match his charming personality. I envied the fact that he didn't need nice clothing to make himself look or feel better, or to fit in at school.

"Well, yo' lil' ass is bad, but not because of what you do at school though," he laughed. "Your mouth pretty bad, and you need to quit sneaking off to the basketball court and do your homework like you're supposed to. And you need to quit cussing at these teachers! Unc told me one of these days he gon' pop you if you keep it up!

"Bro, it's only broke black kids be going in about what everybody wearing. When I did that summer program at that white school, nobody even cared what I wore. I get paid Friday so I'll buy you a couple new shirts aight? You gotta stay outta trouble though," he said.

I nodded, happy about having something new to wear. He knocked me on my head before he got up to go talk Kemis off the ledge.

7

CLAPPING BACK

Without asking my input, Kemis and Pastor D decided I would live out my suspension with Pastor D and his family, something I had done many times before. They seemed to think it would keep me from sneaking off to the basketball court or to hang with my friends. My time away wouldn't have been so bad had Pastor D not said I was on punishment and banned from video games. He also made me go to church on a Wednesday night and pinched me when I fell asleep during service. But the week got better when Sister Robin took me to purchase a new pair of shoes and a few shirts at the mall as a reward for finishing my homework, extra homework, and doing a good job on the chores she had assigned me around the house.

As promised, Jason bought me two shirts. It felt nice to return to school with a couple of new clothing items, which rarely happened in the middle of the school year.

Even with a few new outfits, it didn't stop some kids from saying things about me, prompting me to get another detention a few weeks before Christmas break for "inappropriate language."

An eighth-grade girl was joking about my hair line-up in the hallway, all because I had accidentally bumped into her when backing away from my locker.

"You already black and nappy-headed as hell! Least you can do is stop letting yo' mama do yo' line-up!" she yelled.

I didn't take jokes like that one easily, especially since my own mother had done nothing for me other than give birth. I clapped back at her in front of an audience of adolescents that showed her no empathy.

"Least yo' fat ass can do is lose some fucking weight and grow some edges!"

"Shut up blackie!" she responded before storming off.

The roars of laughter coming from my crew were silenced when my Language Arts teacher told me I would be written up for my language and for bullying. I offered a few choice words to her, considering she heard the entire exchange and was only writing up one of us.

Mr. Mack called home and talked to Kemis, who then took my phone away without even hearing my side of the story. Fortunately, there was no time for an extra-long lecture or extra chores that night since Jason had a basketball game. Pastor D met us at the game and made it a point to sit next to me and discuss Bible verses about mouths and tongues and words while I pretended to listen and nodded my head. I knew that I had said things that I shouldn't, but I thought he made too big a deal about it. He and Kemis didn't seem to agree that her haircut joke justified my response, but they also didn't realize how tired I was of being the center of so many jokes.

8

I GUESS I'M DOING THIS

Even though he despised the idea of me doing anything with my friends, I somehow convinced Kemis to let me hang out the Saturday after my hallway punishment was over. I begged and pleaded and made promises to read and complete homework for the rest of the evening when I returned home, and repeated promises to do my chores without reminders and stop sneaking to the basketball court and to stop cussing out teachers. Even with the promises made, I was allowed to go only under the conditions that Jason took me and watched me the entire time.

The conditions made me feel restricted, like Kemis was again treating me differently than he did Tay, who was able to hang at the mall with his friends all the time. I snarkily reminded him of the fact that Tay was allowed to go to the mall with his friends just one week prior, which didn't change his mind about me.

Jason made it clear he was only agreeing because he needed somewhere to take his new girlfriend, and really was not feeling comfortable with my outing. Once we had picked up his girl and arrived at the mall, I begged him to let me walk with my friends without him baby-sitting me.

"Dude, we just walking around, that's it," I reasoned. "We not doin' anything," I begged.

He had promised Kemis he wouldn't let me out of his sight, and I knew he wouldn't want to risk being in trouble with Kemis if something happened.

"Aight look," he said, "I'ma give you thirty minutes with yo' boys but that's it. Last thing I need is K calling my phone asking to talk to you. You better answer that phone if I call you," he warned me.

"I promise I will. Thanks bro!" I said, and quickly walked away to join up with my friends who were waiting for me in the food court.

After Terrell, Jon, and Josh finished eating, we mostly walked around, window shopped, and occasionally flirted with cute girls we saw. We lingered at the arcade and played a few games, but most of us did not have a lot of money to stay there long, and decided to check out the movie theatre to see what was playing. On the way, we saw a kiosk in the middle of the mall where off-brand and knock-off watches, bags, and sunglasses were sold.

"Yo, Clay, remember how I told you I could get you right? I'm about to hit that up over there. Get you something, and I'll show you how to get some money for it!" Josh said.

I looked down to the kiosk where he had gestured with his head, where a lady sat nearby on a bar height stool reading a book and waiting for customers. She looked like the type that would follow us around as soon as we started showing interest in the merchandise displayed. I assessed the area, noting that there weren't many customers shopping the kiosk, other than the mall walkers who glanced around in passing. Terrell and Jon had already agreed that they wanted in, and I immediately wondered if

I should walk away from them, at the risk of them making fun of me for being afraid, or join in and participate, potentially earning a pay day.

I knew about Josh's new hustle, although I didn't know that his purpose in wanting us all to meet at the mall was so that he could continue with it. I thought we had just been hanging out, and somewhat regretted not thinking it through. He had been stealing like crazy and then selling some of the stuff he stole dirt cheap at school, while other items he took elsewhere. He usually stole from big stores where it seemed no one was ever watching. While none of us were really comfortable with what he was doing, we were all broke, and he was the only one of us that ever had any money.

I found myself agreeing that I would take at least one thing to sell later. We approached the kiosk, where I nervously glanced around before stuffing a handful of watches in my pocket, while Josh quickly grabbed watches, sunglasses, and bracelets, and stuffed them inside his satchel that he wore across his body. Jon and Terrell were reaching and stuffing and repeatedly looking around to see who was watching.

I knew it was a bad idea, and something kept telling me to walk away without participating, but I figured I would just do it once and then never again, thinking I could get some money out of it to save for a pair of Nike sweatpants like my friends all had. I couldn't shake that feeling of guilt that overcame me. It was that feeling Pastor D had talked about before, but I did my best to ignore it while the four of us tried to casually slip away from the scene of the crime.

"Hey hey hey!" The lady working the kiosk yelled as we all walked off. "Get back here! Security!"

Our walk immediately transformed into a sprint, and we traversed a long stretch of the mall before deciding to split up and meet down the street at the bus stop. It was an irrational plan for me since I had to find Jason, but knew I had to escape without Jason knowing what I did. As laid back as he was, even he would have thrashed me if he knew I had stolen something when he was supposed to be watching me. The four of us split into two groups and fled to two different bus stops that were each a little under a mile from the mall. Terrell and I sprinted across a four-lane road dodging traffic and ran toward the eastbound bus stop that was headed toward the train station.

He smiled in relief once the bus squealed off and we found seats near the back. "C, you fast as hell, dude," he said in between breaths. "Ain't nobody catching you!"

"You think security came after us? I ain't even see no one," I said, still catching my breath as well.

"I ain't see nobody either. I think we good. Josh crazy dawg."

As we neared the train station, my phone started buzzing, and I panicked upon seeing that Jason was calling.

"Jay, don't trip. Rel wanted to show me something at his crib. We on the train." I lied about our whereabouts but was stepping off of the bus at the train station as I spoke.

"Clay, are you cappin' right now? Get off at the next stop so I can pick y'all up. You out here trying to get my keys took again! Where you gon' be?"

"The South Station," I told him, wondering if he would punch me in the face when he saw me.

"I'm on my way," he said before ending the call.

Jason was waiting for us at the train station when we got off the train, and he drove off without a word after we climbed into the car from the sidewalk.

"Where yo' girl go?" I asked him, seeing that she was no longer with him.

"I already dropped her off, bro," he told me in a low voice between gritted teeth.

He kept his gaze straight ahead with a sour expression. He drove to Terrell's house without a word but unleashed once Terrell was safely in his house and out of earshot.

"What the hell was y'all doing?" Jason grilled me once we were alone.

"I told you!" I exclaimed.

"I know you lying to me. We heard some people in the mall talking about four boys that was stealing and got chased out!" he yelled.

"That wasn't us! Josh and Jon left before we did," I said, hoping he didn't detect the lie.

He didn't ask any more questions, but when we pulled up to the house, he beat me to my car door and opened it to let me out the car. As soon as I stepped onto the sidewalk, he forcefully reached down into my pockets, shifting my entire body forward, and pulled out the watches I had taken.

"Jay, that's not—"

Before I could finish offering my excuse, his free hand had knocked me across the top of my forehead.

"Ah, bro!"

He followed with a barrage of punches to my arms and stomach before stopping to hurl additional threats. "I should tell K so he can beat the shit out yo' ass!"

"You dead ass? Cause I ain't never snitched on you!" I said while grasping my arms, hoping he didn't plan on continuing his attack once we got inside.

He stood on the sidewalk looking away from me like he wasn't sure what he was going to do next, and finally clicked the keys to lock the car and stuffed the watches into his pockets.

"I ain't taking you to the mall ever again. Get inside!" he said.

I huffed into the house, mad that he had taken my only chances of making any money. But Josh texted in the group chat that night a message that encouraged me to not give up on the watches. He assured me that if I got them back, he could get me some money for them. When I asked him how, he told us that when he stole something of good quality, he took the items to a guy called Flip who would pay him on the spot, depending upon what he brought. I made a deal with Josh that I would start bringing items for him to take to Flip, and he could keep five dollars from each transaction.

I snuck to Jason's room the next day after he had gone to work and Daveon went out to a friend's house, and I rummaged through Jason's things until I located the watches. I was relieved to find them and pack them in my backpack to transfer to Josh that Monday.

9

I THINK I LIKE THIS

At school, I gave Josh the watches with a promise from him that he would text me as soon as he saw Flip.

"If you looking for something else to hit up, that General Sports on Florissant is so easy. They don't even chase nobody. I can't go in there since I've stole too many times, and they recognize my face. They would let you in though. And ain't no way they'd catch *you* anyway," he told me.

The store wasn't too far from our house, and only a few minutes' walk from my school bus stop. I contemplated on how I could get it done while I was with Tay and knew I couldn't. Although Tay would never snitch on me, I knew he wouldn't let me run off to a store and steal either.

Skipping out of school before my last class that day and catching the city bus to the store seemed to be my best option since students could ride free when presenting a student identification. I successfully slipped out the front doors of the school without being noticed by one of the security guards and rode the bus to my destination without incident.

The sidewalk in front of the store had a few loiterers, making me nervous to rest my backpack against the brick wall outside the entry way to the store. I knew I would have to in order to keep from raising the suspicions of the workers inside. I was overwhelmed with the options of items to steal once inside, especially since there were multiple displays loaded with shirts that I wanted to take for myself. I instead settled on a pair of shoes, knowing they would likely yield a greater return than a shirt.

A girl who was working approached me to ask if I needed help. I asked her if they had shoes on sale, feeling they would suspect something if I asked for an expensive pair. She led me to a table of shoes toward the back of the store that had a clearance sign posted at the front of the table and left me alone while she tended to some items on the other side of the store. I scanned the table, checking the prices for the most expensive pair I could find, and once I settled for a pricey pair to take, I slowly lifted them out of the box, pretended to perform a thorough examination, and nervously checked around the store to see who was watching.

The girl who had helped me glanced over at me, and I put the shoes down and picked up a different pair, pretending to assess their quality. Once she seemed preoccupied with another customer, I picked up the expensive pair and began my race toward the doors. I had already scooped up my backpack and was down the sidewalk before one of the workers ran out of the store to confront me. I had sprinted to freedom and ran past my street into an alley where I stuffed the shoes inside my backpack and waited to meet Tay at the bus stop.

"Bro, where you been? You know I'm not allowed to come home without you!" Tay reminded me after he stepped off the bus.

"Chill, Tay. I just had to handle something after school," I said.

"Dude, did you get in another fight?"

"Naw, bro!" I said.

"Did you go smoke? If you did I ain't trying to walk in the house with you and K smell it and wonder if it was me," Tay said.

"Bro, chill. I haven't smoked nothing. Besides you would smell it now. It ain't even like that. If K ask, just tell him I rode the bus home with you, aight?"

Tay shook his head. "If I get caught lying and get my ass whooped for you again, you better do my chores for a month!" he said.

"Aight, but ain't nobody about to get caught," I said, realizing that I had spoken those words nearly every time we had gotten caught.

I thought my plan had gone perfectly until I got home from the basketball court later and Kemis called me down into his room to talk. I figured he was about to go in on me for running off to ball again without my homework being finished, but he instead started grilling me about skipping my last class that day. He had gotten an email from the teacher and the principal.

"I was gonna go, but I had to take a dump!" I told him, hoping he would believe I had uncontrollable bodily functions, at least enough to keep my phone out of his hands.

"Why didn't you go afterwards?" he asked.

"I was still using it! My stomach was hurting!" I told him. He cocked his head to the side and pursed his lips before standing up from the bed and letting out a deep sigh.

"Clay, I don't know what you were doing during your class, but I know there ain't that much daggone constipation in the world that would keep you in the bathroom for a whole damn hour. Don't let it happen again or I'm grabbing yo' phone again. Go do your homework cause Unc on his way to talk to you," he said.

The last thing I wanted was to face homework and another Bible lecture, but I had to endure both before I was allowed any peace that night. The next day was better, since Josh handed me twenty dollars for the watches I had taken, and I handed him the shoes I had stolen for him to take to Flip.

"These lit! I can't believe you snatched these!" he said with a smile on his face. I proudly recounted the details of how I got away with it and beamed when he told me I would probably get even more money than I got from the watches.

Class time became my primary time to look for more places to go and steal from. I knew I couldn't keep stealing from neighborhood stores since my brothers knew too many people, and word would eventually travel back home. Josh suggested I wait until after Christmas, since a lot of stores had extra security around the holidays, but he told me it was a good time to rummage through unlocked cars in mall parking lots, which was how he planned to spend his break.

10

DRIP DROP

"**B**ro, lemme get that off you!"

I was a new person when I returned to school after Christmas break. I had new clothes to show off after spending nearly a week with Pastor D and Sister Robin, who had purchased more items for me than I had ever been gifted in my life. I had also purchased myself a new name-brand shirt with my shoe and watch money. On top of that, during the break, Josh had begun meeting me at Jason's games since his team had played in a few holiday tournaments, and I would sneak out of the gym and the two of us would search for unlocked vehicles in the parking lot to find money and other items. Since Flip had started paying fifty dollars for stolen credit cards, we had taken advantage of a few unexpectedly large pay days.

Between the cash I took from cars and the money from Flip in exchange for credit cards and other items, I had amassed enough money to make regular wardrobe updates outside of our lockers. The compliments I received and the fact that I was no longer being teased for my clothing and shoes fueled my desire to gather more, especially after Lakisha told me in the hallway one day that I had been looking fresh.

"Nigga it's new! I ain't hardly wore it yet!" Terrell said. He normally let me buy some of his things, understanding that Jason was still refusing to take me to the mall after our last incident.

"Bruh chill, I'll pay you for it. I ain't saying I want it free!" I defended, knowing it usually didn't take a huge offering of cash before he parted with something new. Although he had more cash to make purchases, most of the clothing items he wore were stolen, and he would sell it to me for a small amount, knowing he could easily replace it.

It had become a normal part of our hallway time to buy things before class. But even when we conducted our business quickly, it was difficult to arrive at class on time since Josh and I were often stealing from the school's snack store in between classes. Josh had stolen the key to the store from one of the janitors, and we found it easier than expected to get into the cash register to take money, but also to take items in the store to munch on during class.

But getting into the snack store and conducting hallway transactions often kept me in the hallway longer than I should have been, especially with teachers who seemed eager to write me up when I arrived late. And since my brother had been threatening to take my phone if I got written up too many times, I figured it was time to conduct more of my activities after school so that I could avoid being late to any classes. I had no choice but to explain my activities to Tay so that I could steal after school while my brothers thought I was at the basketball court.

Thanks to Tay reluctantly swearing not to rat me out, on a day where we had stashed some items for Flip in Terrell's room, Terrell, Jon, and I decided to hit up a liquor store not far from Terrell's house, knowing we could get cash from Flip if we successfully stole bottles of alcohol.

"Bro, you promised you wouldn't be gone long!" Tay said. I was checking in with him on the phone while the three of us walked toward our destination.

"Chill, Tay! You told them I was at the court, right?" I asked.

"Yeah, but Day already went down there looking for you, and now Jay going! You better hurry up before K get home!" he warned.

"They ain't gon' snitch me out to K, bro. We ain't gon' be that long. I gotta go but I'll text you when I'm on the way," I said as we reached the store.

As suspected, our young faces and small frames caused us to be shouted at as soon as we walked in, and we knew we had to move quickly.

"Ay! Y'all kids not allowed to purchase anything in here without being twenty-one! If there's something you want, you gon' have to bring your parents back!" an older man shouted from behind the plexiglass at the counter.

The three of us looked at each other just before we each snatched and stuffed as many bottles as we could and raced outside and all the way to Terrell's house. We closed the door to Terrell's room and opened up one of the bottles to pass around between the three of us and Terrell's cousin, all while trying to not raise the suspicions of Terrell's grandmother.

We were trashed within minutes, and sent drunken texts and social media messages to our girl crushes, posed for pictures we knew we would need to erase, and talked and laughed and stumbled around Terrell's room while Terrell joked about how terrible Jon and I were with "holding liquor." Eventually Josh came through with his cousin we called Wood, along with Flip, who we handed the unopened bottles in exchange for cash. I vaguely remembered that Josh's cousin Wood offered me a ride home, which I took knowing that Jason was likely upset when he didn't find me at the basketball court.

I was only slightly less dizzy when I stumbled into the apartment, hoping I could lie down without heckling from my brothers.

"Where you been and why the hell you ain't been answering yo' phone?" Jason asked something along those lines once I walked in. I couldn't make out everything he said, but I could tell by his tone I was in trouble with him.

"Big bro…you ain't call me," I slurred, trying my best to conceal my intoxication by putting my hand over my mouth, hoping it would hide any odor of alcohol that could escape from my breath.

He immediately looked at me like I was crazy. "Shit, bro. You been drinking? K gon' fucking kill you when he get home. He out looking for you after I couldn't find you at the court! Come on!" He practically carried me up to my bed and helped me get my clothes off. "You want a sandwich?" he asked after seeing how out of sorts I was.

"Mmhmm," I grumbled as I pulled my blanket up to my ears. I didn't remember much after that, other than scarfing down the sandwich, and waking up in the middle of the night and hovering over Tay's bed to vomit it up.

11

A MINOR EXPLOSION

It took a lot of convincing to get Tay to lie for me again and say I was at the basketball court when my crew and I boldly returned to the mall for our next mission, with a plan to remove cell phones from a cell phone store. Josh handed us each a box cutter after we left the metro bus stop.

"I stole these from the hardware store," he said.

"Damn nigga, where ain't you stole from?" Jon joked.

"Bruh, some of these stores make it so easy. This store in here is a little harder though. You gotta lift up the phone and cut the wire underneath it to get the phone loose. But Flip be paying hella for a new phone, 'cause he send them off to somebody that reprogram 'em," said Josh.

"How many times you done this?" I asked.

"None, nigga! Flip told me how to do it!" Josh said.

"They gon' know something up if we all go in there together," Terrell said, thinking about how we could actually pull off Josh's plan.

"T, you should go in first and distract one of the workers. Ask for a phone to look at or something, we'll run in and cut the phones out. When you see us running, you run—we'll just split all the money," I said.

"Nigga you act like you our leader or something!" Josh said.

"Chill, nigga! He the only one that came up with something!" Terrell said.

"Right! Otherwise, we gon' be caught," Jon added.

I hadn't appreciated Josh's outburst, but set it aside so we could quickly finish what we needed to do. We all pulled up our hoodies before entering the mall and tried to slowly file into the area where the phone store was located. Josh sat on a bench in front of the store to watch Terrell in action, while Jon and I stood off to the side pretending to window shop. Once we saw that Terrell had successfully occupied an employee, he gave us the signal, and we went in to work.

The hardest part was staying focused when I could tell that shoppers around us had noticed we had cut multiple cell phones down from the displays and thrown them into the bags we carried.

"Yo, what are they doing?" a man inquired nearby.

"Hey!" Stop!" someone screamed.

Without looking up, I threw the last phone in my bag and turned to run, bursting into and nearly knocking over an older lady who was browsing the table directly behind where I had been. I joined up with the rest of the crew, who had already made it out of the store, and was far ahead of them by the time I reached the entry doors to the mall. I knew I couldn't stop once I stepped outside and felt nervous about running to the same bus stop that I ran to the first time we had stolen. I instead decided to run through a neighborhood adjacent to the mall and take a different bus home instead of the train.

I placed the bag of phones on the ground next to the front stoop when I arrived home, knowing I would be receiving death stares when I walked into the apartment. I slowly opened the door after turning the key to find Daveon and Tay in the front room eating a plate of dinner while watching television.

"Bro, where you been dude?" Daveon asked as though he knew I wouldn't have a valid excuse to offer.

"I was at the court!" I said. "What y'all eating?"

"You wasn't at no court, bro. We checked, and K out looking for you! You need to quit worrying about what we eating and worry about putting on extra underwear before he get home!"

"He pissed?" I asked, afraid that I actually needed to take Daveon's advice seriously.

"Hell yeah! He said he asked around and nobody at the court saw you or yo' boys the whole day! Where was you at for real? Hold up, this him again." Daveon rolled his eyes before picking up his phone from next to him on the couch. "K, he here…aight…bye. You done bro. Ay where you—"

I quickly ran outside to the porch to retrieve my bag of cell phones and bolted up the steps to my room, locking the door and digging deep into the bottom of the closet to conceal the phones I had taken. Once I felt satisfied with the hiding spot, I took Daveon's advice and began throwing on every clean pair of underwear I had in my drawer. When I found that there were only four pairs, I dug into the hamper, throwing clothes around until I found some unclean ones to add on before throwing my pants back on.

I strolled down the steps and to the kitchen with confidence to warm up a plate of dinner that I had missed. The microwave had just finished the final beep when the front door shot open.

"For real Clay? Where you been?" I wasn't sure if he skipped, hopped or flew, but it seemed that it took him no time at all to advance from the doorway to within two inches of my face, threatening my life with his expression.

"Chill, K! I was at the court!" I thought keeping a casual tone would convince him to do the same, but I quickly found that I was wrong.

"You a 'at the court' lie, Clay! We all been to the court looking for you! Ain't nobody seen you at the court all day! And you were supposed to have your ass in the house, knowing daggone well you on punishment since that last little stunt! And you ain't done a lick of homework!" he yelled.

"I ain't really have that much homework today!" I said.

"Bro, you think I ain't check your homework portal? You have plenty of homework tonight, homework that you didn't do! You weren't doing your work, and you weren't at the court, so where the hell were you?" he roared.

By then I had taken a bite of food, and I was hoping he would at least let me finish chewing before demanding an answer. My hopes were diminished when he slightly pushed my shoulder with his fingertips, again demanding an answer.

"I said where the hell were you, bro?" he asked.

"Why you all up in my damn face when I'm tryna eat?" I asked in efforts to deflect.

"Bro I don't give a damn about you trying to eat! You shoulda been here at dinner if you wanted to eat!" he yelled.

Without warning, he snatched my plate and threw it in the trash. Seeing my pasta thrown away made me seethe, and I wanted more than anything for him to lose it as much as I had. I stood up and jump kicked the trash can, sending it flying across the room until its contents spread out, leaving red pasta sauce stains streaming across the wall and the floor underneath it.

The expression on my brother's face when he glared at me told me everything I needed to know about his intentions before he announced them.

"Bro I'm 'bout to—"

He beelined towards me before finishing his threat, and I stormed out of the kitchen and shot through the front room, only briefly flashing in front of Daveon's view of the television before flying up the steps to my room with Kemis directly behind me, already wildly swinging his fists and connecting to my legs and backside, causing me to nearly trip and fall on the stairway. He rested his fists when he started swinging a belt, making it harder for me to escape, and easier for me to feel I was not receiving the protection I wanted from my excess underwear.

"Bro chill!" I yelled while crawling underneath my blanket and trying to grab his belt at the same time.

"Naw, *you* gon' chill, bro! I'm done with yo' bad ass act—"

"Kemis! Whoa whoa whoa! Aht aht gimme that!" I was relieved when Pastor D ran into the room and stood between Kemis and me. "What is going on?"

"UNC! He just got home after all this time…remember when I called you earlier? He been out kicking it with his boys and been gone for hours, coming in lying saying he was at the basketball court, lying about his homework, cussing at me, and then kicked the trashcan spilling food all over the damn floor!" Kemis yelled.

"He cussing at me and he threw my fucking dinner away and I ain't even get to eat yet!" I yelled back, still out of breath and clutching my body from the blows he had dealt.

"Cause I was trying to talk to you and you acted like you could use dinner to be hella disrespectful!" he said.

"Okay okay, fellas, come on. Kemis, son, please go to your room and calm down," Pastor D said. Kemis sighed deeply and backtracked out of the room with his fists still balled up.

Pastor D slowly walked to the door and locked it, placed the belt he had confiscated on top of the dresser, and returned to join me on the bed, resting his elbows on top of his knees while I slowly pushed the blanket off of my bottom half.

"Clay," he spoke softly before even looking in my direction, "your brother has been worried to death all afternoon. He called me hours ago and has been out looking for you since Tay walked in the house without you. And you've once again been disobedient by not coming straight home. It's too much, Clay!" He sighed and rubbed his head in his face as though he was formulating his words. "Where have you been? And don't lie and say the basketball court."

I looked away, taking time to make a believable lie that wouldn't provoke him to allow Kemis to come and finish me off. "I just went to my boy house to play this game."

"I don't feel like you're telling me the truth." He responded that way often, but strangely, only when I was bold-faced lying to him. He had never said it when I told the truth, and it was scary to think he was capable of discerning the difference. Still, I had no choice but to continue in what I had started, knowing that even he wouldn't remain composed if I shared my actual whereabouts.

"I knew I shouldn't'a went but I'm tired of being on punishment and having to sit at home and just do homework!"

"Tired of being on punishment? Clay, you recently skipped school, left the house when you weren't supposed to, and showed up at home intoxicated! He said you haven't been getting your work turned in, and I see why if you still sneaking off to that basketball court! You need to be thinking about what got you on punishment in the first place and change your behavior around. You better thank God Almighty that you're not a resident of my home. And your Granny would have got your little behind if she were still here!"

I did not want any reminders of Granny in that moment, especially the reminders that involved the times I stressed her out with getting into so much trouble. She was not with us, and I deeply hated life without her.

"Clay Deontay Lands, you were in the wrong to come home late, and talk crazy to your brother and kick over that trash can like that. You need to go downstairs and clean up the mess you made. Then get yourself some dinner and bring it up here and get your work done while I go talk to your brother. I don't want to hear of you speaking to your brother in that manner anymore, do you understand?" he asked.

I nodded and got up to do what I was told, feeling like I should do at least one right thing for the day after an evening of doing a lot of bad. I hadn't meant for things to escalate the way they had, or to get Kemis so angry, and definitely had not intended for Pastor D to have to come over and bring order, as he had done many times in the past. I figured I would need a new way to make money with my friends if my brother planned to explode when I didn't come home after school.

12

FAT POCKETS

Knowing we could only steal so much during daylight hours without someone eventually recognizing our faces and without my brother taking my life, the crew made plans for late night excursions to apartment complexes across town, where we usually found goldmines of unlocked cars in unattended parking lots, with unexpecting victims. I knew there was no way Jason and Daveon would let me sneak out of their window, so I gave money to Flip for a fire escape rope ladder that I could attach to the window in my room. It was the benefit of becoming a favorite of Josh's plug, who would order nearly anything from online in exchange for some of the stolen goods I was bringing.

Sometimes Flip would reward me with a pair of shoes or jewelry or extra money to keep that he would call my "bonuses" for bringing him so many items, more than anyone else in the crew. Some of the bonuses I would share with Josh, who seemed to be uncomfortable with the fact that Flip had started meeting up with me at school or at the bus stop to make our exchanges, completely eliminating my need for Josh to be our middle man.

Some of those bonuses went straight to Tay, who I had to plead with and bribe to keep him quiet about what I was doing. Every time I went somewhere, I had promised him it was the last time I was going to steal, but then subsequently broke the promise. I started regularly giving him money for snacks at school in hopes that he would keep quiet and not get tempted to tell Daveon or Jason about my affairs.

Our second late-night mission almost became our last. The four of us caught two buses, each carrying only a small backpack to our location, which was the parking lot of a large apartment building in a neighborhood better-off than our own. We laughed at all the belongings people would leave in unlocked vehicles— vehicle keys, cellular phones, and large sums of cash. I chuckled but then panicked when I stumbled across a loaded pistol lying atop the driver's seat in a luxury vehicle.

"Bruh! You keeping that? The OG will pay a couple hunned for it!" Josh said as we strolled toward a nearby bus stop at nearly two in the morning after we were done for the night.

"For real? Damn, I was gon' keep it, but I might go 'head and sell it then!" I said, thinking about the risks of one of my brothers finding out I had brought home a firearm. Shortly after I had stuffed it back inside my bag, I noticed the others had frozen in place on the sidewalk, staring ahead of us. When I looked up my eyes met a brightly colored, marked police vehicle rounding the corner.

"Shit! Meet at the spot!" Josh yelled, prompting the four of us to quickly separate and sprint until we could safely meet at our previously agreed upon location.

My arms pumped me far enough away until the sounds of my sneakers patting the pavement was all I heard besides the uninvited thoughts in my brain telling me I was about to be arrested. I quickly flew across an open field, hearing hardly anything other than the wind that gripped my ears before I stretched the sides of my hood downward as far as it could reach. By the time I looked back, I didn't see anyone or anything except the flashes from the police lights reflecting off of a nearby building, and wondered if my crew had all gotten away.

I continued on until I reached a fenced construction area surrounded by hotels and a few closed shops and restaurants. After reassuring myself there were no officers around, I threw my bag over the fence and scaled it, snatched up my bag on the other side, and climbed up into the cab of a large bulldozer, where I hunched down on top of steel plates and texted the crew to see if everyone was in the clear. All but Jon responded that they were good to go.

On my way to meet the others, a dark car pulled up alongside me, almost prompting me to run before the occupants called me.

"Get in bruh! Found this shit wit' the keys in it!" Josh yelled from the driver's seat. I laughed in disbelief before climbing into the backseat behind Terrell, hoping we would actually make it home without being arrested for a curfew violation or worse.

Tay had let down the escape ladder in time for me to crawl up to safety in my room. I was thankful that I had made it home in one piece, and without a police escort, unlike Jon, who had been caught not far from where we had been standing when we first saw the police vehicle. He had at least been smart enough to throw his phone while he ran, which likely shielded the rest of us from detection later on. The police recovered his bag of stolen items that he dropped while he ran, and took him home to his mother at nearly three in the morning. He told us at school that he was on punishment, but it didn't stop him from rejoining us the next week.

We weren't able to sneak across town as often as we liked, as we found out the metro bus drivers were suspicious of pre-teen boys traveling on buses in the middle of the night. Some of them would ask where we were going, or "where yo' mamas at?" But after seeing how much money we were making, Josh's cousin Wood offered us rides if we gave him a cut of our money. Our escapades become easier, but keeping Tay on my side and keeping my other brothers from finding out what I was into felt more challenging than ever.

13

CATCHING UP AND
CATCHING TROUBLE

"Clay, if I have to come in this room one more time, I promise you bro!"

Kemis had regularly fussed at me on mornings before school about getting out of bed and getting out the door on time to catch the bus. Our daily battle generally included multiple threats of bodily harm, some of which he followed through on when he returned to the room for the third or fourth time and found me still lying in the bed. This particular morning was after an especially late night out with my crew. We had hit jackpot at a local casino parking lot and found more spoils than any other time we had been out, prompting us to stay later and not miss out on any opportunities. It felt as though I had just laid down when Kemis was waking me up for school.

"Damn, bro! Why you gotta be on some extra shit today!" I shouted after my backside hit the floor from Kemis dragging me out of bed by my ankles.

"Boy I know you not in here speaking to your brother like that!" Pastor D said.

I looked up, startled to see Pastor D standing in the doorway behind Kemis. He often came by to bring Kemis breakfast after the rest of us had gotten off to school, but I wished I had an advanced warning of his presence.

"Unc, it ain't like that!" was all I could muster in defense of my language.

"Sounds just like that! Get your behind up and go brush your teeth!" he said. I struggled to my feet and moped off to the bathroom, less willing to disobey Pastor D than I was my brother.

I was living with the downsides of staying out late to make more money than I had ever possessed. Not only would Kemis refuse to let me sleep in and be great, but my teachers also wouldn't let me use their boring instruction time to catch up on sleep either. While my friends had the luxury of simply staying home when they were tired, Kemis was not a fan of us missing school.

Two of my teachers, the teachers whose classes were most boring anyway, both wrote me up that same week for falling asleep in class multiple times. I found myself back in the principal's office after the write-ups and seemed to have successfully convinced him that I wasn't sleeping at night because of the nightmares I was having about Granny. That plan only backfired, as Principal Mack, with the agreement of my brother, began forcing me to see the guidance counselor once a week, which was even more tortuous than the boring classes I had been sleeping in.

I tried harder to mask how tired I was, and only became more frustrated and more mouthy when my efforts didn't work. I was back to saying whatever I wanted without considering the consequences that I knew would come, particularly since my clothes were much fresher, the teasing had mostly subsided, and I hardly minded being the center of attention. In fact, I found it refreshing, since I had gained popularity for looking good instead of looking rough, and had garnered a reputation for always having money and nice things.

Although I had found the favor of my peers, my teachers continued to be unimpressed with me. After growing tired of my mouthiness, my teachers began reaching out to Kemis again, who grew more upset with each bad report. Pastor D had been over one night after my science teacher had called Kemis to tell him about our interaction that day when I had fallen asleep in class again. She had decided to give me one of those "I want to make sure everything is okay at home" type talks in front of the entire class. Her speech ended with words I didn't appreciate.

"Clay, your grades can't afford for you to sleep through any more class time!"

"Well, I wouldn't sleep if you taught some shit worth staying awake for!" I yelled, prompting the class to erupt in laughter and her to erupt in anger. I hadn't meant to get everyone laughing, but I didn't like that she gave out hints about my grade in front of everyone.

She wrote me up and told me to sit in the principal's office for the remainder of class.

She additionally told Kemis that during the class times when I wasn't sleeping, I had been disruptive and was taking pictures with my friends. I was in the middle of explaining that she was lying because she didn't like me when Pastor D unexpectedly snatched my phone and started browsing through it.

"Unc, come on! Why you gotta—"

"Boy you better watch your tone! What are you upset about? If she's lying, we'll be able to see," he said.

I grew silent thinking of how I had forgotten to erase the photos I had been taking in class and kept my head down while

Kemis and Pastor D viewed all of the evidence that corroborated my teacher's report.

"So, you just gon' lie dead in my face, huh?" Kemis asked.

"That's exactly what he did. Clay, what exactly do you think class time is for? You think it's for taking selfies? And where is all this money from that you and your friends are posing with?" Pastor D asked.

I couldn't think of an answer he could possibly find acceptable, especially after knowing I had behaved badly and tried to cover it up with a lie.

I continued with another lie with hopes to get them to stop focusing on everything I had done and the wads of cash they saw in the pictures. "Unc, it's fake. And I know what class time is for. But like, even when people have jobs, don't they get to take breaks and stuff? Y'all go to work without stopping?"

"Clay Lands, don't try me. You get a lunch break, and you all go outside after lunch. You get almost ten minutes in between classes, and you hardly do anything in art and gym. Your classes are only forty-five or fifty minutes. And even with all that, you only there for seven hours. By the way, I went all day today without one selfie, and you can stand to wait until you get home!" he responded.

"Can I just have my phone?" I asked.

"Boy? If you were in my home this phone would be gone until school was out!" Pastor D said.

Kemis followed by telling me that he was keeping my phone, and I struggled to stay awake while they both lectured me at the kitchen table for nearly an hour that night. Other than sleep, all I could think about while they talked was all the money that I would miss out on if I couldn't talk to my friends and to Flip.

14

SMOKE AND FIRE

The lecturing from Pastor D and my brother didn't stop me from getting suspended three times the next month, despite my hard-core efforts to stay out of trouble and keep my phone in my possession once it was returned. The first suspension was for another fight. Josh and I had been outside after lunch when a kid named Drashawn, who had ongoing beef with Josh, saw the two of us and approached us with all of his friends around.

Our crew had a growing list of enemies, primarily consisting of kids who had stated their family members' cars had gotten broken into, as word had somehow spread about our activities, which had escalated from just entering unlocked vehicles to the occasional breaking out of windows to get into locked cars as well. Drashawn had already been mad with Josh after his girlfriend abruptly decided she wanted to be Josh's girl instead of his. But when he approached us after lunch, he accused Josh and me of stealing from his locker. While I knew I hadn't stolen anything from him, I wasn't exactly sure if Josh had done so or not, but still adamantly denied the allegations, while Josh hardly said a word.

"I should kick yo' ass for stealing from me," Drashawn said.

"Do what you gotta do or step," I told him, not really wanting to fight about something I was hardly involved in.

"What you say, nigga?" he asked, stepping even closer to my face.

"I think you heard me, bruh! If you gon' swing, swing! But I think you know betta!"

All his friends looked to him as if they expected for him to finish what he had started. I was willing and ready to walk away, and had even motioned to Josh that we should ignore him and move along. But Drashawn made an announcement that completely set me off.

"I ain't even trippin. Y'all gotta steal from me cause y'all broke as hell, and only got nice shit cause y'all bought that shit on EBT…broke ass busted ass niggas!"

I had worked too hard to put the reputation of being broke behind me to allow him to restart rumors that could cause me to be the target of everyone's jokes again. I told him in certain words to back off. Instead of listening, he pushed me, and in front of a crowd that had accumulated after seeing commotion, yelled, "Fight, you little black ass, broke ass nigga!" followed with another push.

"Bruh, I see what it is," I told him after stumbling back. "You just need some money don't you?" I reached in my pocket and threw a handful of ten-dollar bills into the air over his head and watched them rain down around him.

He made the mistake of stooping down to grab a few bills off the pavement, and I seized the opportunity to do exactly what he had requested and pummeled his face in, feeling that he had come for me since I was smaller than Josh. After noticing blood gushing from his face, his friends tried to push me off of him, prompting Josh to start pushing them away to keep the fight fair, but they didn't stop until I started swinging in their direction and connecting. I continued until the security guards broke through the crowd and escorted Drashawn and his bloody face to the nurse's office and escorted me to the principal's office.

The scene inside the principal's office became almost as volatile as the fight outside after Drashawn arrived with a cut over his eye and a busted lip, eyeing me angrily like he wanted another try.

"Nigga you betta quit staring at me 'fore I make you even uglier," I said.

"Ain't nobody uglier than yo' black ass! I'll clip you so hard you'll turn purple, bitch ass nigga!" he said.

"Hey hey! Fellas, that language is unacceptable! The two of you are in enough trouble as it is. Clay, your brother is not going to be happy to hear from me again, and neither is your mother, Drashawn. Now which one of you hit first?" he asked.

We nearly got into another fight after Drashawn accused me of hitting him first, causing Principal Mack to jump from his seat and hold me while he ordered Drashawn to move to the opposite end of the room.

"Clay, go ahead out and gather up your backpack and your homework. Your teachers are expecting you," Mr. Mack said while walking me to the door to make sure nothing else happened.

After gathering my homework, I encountered Drashawn's angry mother in the hallway outside the principal's office when I was returning, griping about how Drashawn had not done anything and shouldn't be getting suspended from school. She abruptly stopped her speech upon seeing me.

"Is that the lil' bad ass boy that started this shit?" she asked Principal Mack. A nearly three-inch, green and blue, curvy nail was pointed at me while she rested her other hand on her hip and cocked her head to the side, awaiting an answer from the principal.

"Yo' crackhead ass don't even know me like that!" I responded, hoping to offend both her and Drashawn.

"That's enough, young man!" I was shocked to see Pastor D pop his head into the hallway and tug my arm while correcting me for my speech.

"Disrespectful ass little kids! Is this yo' son?" she yelled with an even more irate tone at Pastor D.

"Mr. Farmer, you all can wait for me in my office. I'll be there shortly," Mr. Mack said. I reluctantly followed Pastor D back into the office, wondering what he had already been told about my day. "Mr. Lands," Principal Mack started after entering the room shortly after I sat down, "apparently your brother is in a lengthy meeting this afternoon, so he sent Pastor Dwayne, who is on your emergency notification list. You'll be going home with him. I told him and your brother that the behavioral intervention team has reached out, pointing out that you have had multiple acts of violence at this school, Clay. They have inquired if you would be better served at our alternative school in the district. They are right that you have had multiple suspensions and multiple fights since you started middle school. However, I told them you're very intelligent, although your grades and your behavior don't always reflect that. Let me just encourage you to turn your behavior around before the decision is no longer mine to make."

I rolled my eyes, not caring where I went to school every day. School was school, and wherever it was, I didn't want to be there.

"Do they got a basketball team?" I nonchalantly asked.

Principal Mack sighed and turned to look at Pastor D, who thanked him for his time and told him we would be going.

"I know what you thinking, but this wasn't even my fault!" I said to Pastor D after he started driving out of the parking lot and starting in on his lecture.

He gave me that "boy please" look. "Tell me why you think so," he said.

I knew he wasn't going to be interested in what I had to say, but I decided to try anyway. "Bruh—"

"I'm not your bruh," he cut me off before I could tell my story.

"Unc, he got up in my face and started going in on me, and then he pushed me!"

"Tell me what you said to him between him getting in your face and the push, and I want an exact quote," he said.

I got just a little smart with him. "If I give you an exact quote, you gon' get that stupid dictionary from K room when we get home."

He smiled. "Okay, you can tell me exactly what you said with no consequences, no matter what it was," he said.

I hesitated. One time Granny promised the same thing and she still smacked me.

"'Back the fuck up before I drop you on this pavement,'" I quoted, using the same volume and tone I had used earlier.

His eyes widened. and he bit down on his lip. "So would you classify your statement as soft words or as a harsh tongue?" he asked.

I was annoyed that he was going to biblically analyze everything I did. Fortunately, he had parked his van in the parking lot at home, saving me from answering what I deemed was an unfair question.

I didn't expect Kemis to be too upset about the fight, as long as he was convinced that I didn't start it. He had just ended his meeting and looked like he was already stressed when he sat with Pastor D and me in the kitchen.

"So, we're suspended again, Clay?" he asked.

I was frustrated at his willingness to categorize the suspension with all the others, and pled my case to him that he always said we could defend ourselves. He let up after that, but of course still had to voice his disapproval.

"You really can't afford any more suspensions, Clay. You done missed too much school. I understand if someone is punching you, you gotta do what you gotta do. But sometimes you have to be the bigger and more mature person and walk away," he said.

"C'mon, bro. When I was little, you never told me that. Plus, I saw you fight a bunch of times. And you got suspended from school for fighting. You ain't walk away! You dropped hella niggas on the street!" I said, feeling the need to remind him of everything I had grown up watching him do.

"Watch the language, Clay!" said Pastor D.

"Clay, those times in the neighborhood was usually because of something Jason or Day had gotten going, and I was showing up for them. Plus, I was a different person then. You'll see one day—the last thing you want to have to do when you're applying for college is discuss all of your suspensions," he said.

"Not interested in college anymore…it's just more school. And new Kemis is lame," I said as I got up to leave.

15

HAVE NOTS

I was eager to sneak out that night, knowing I wouldn't have to be up crazy early for school since I was suspended. Wood drove us to a popular casino where we quickly became spooked when we kept spotting the same white security jeep with flashing lights creep behind us every time we shifted to a different section of the lot. After circling a few more times we aborted the casino mission to try the parking lot of a posh hotel across town, where we found exactly what we were looking for.

Wood idled toward the rear of the lot with the headlights off and remained in the driver's seat as our lookout while the four of us split up to scavenge the lot for targets. After spending nearly twenty minutes going through cars, Josh alerted us to a locked Chevy where we could see a wad of cash and a wallet resting on top of the driver's seat through the front window, and he decided to get a crowbar from Wood's car to break in.

"Yo you sure, bruh?" Jon asked. "This spot is pretty close. Someone might hear and look out the window!"

"We ain't gon' get caught bruh. Y'all can wait in the car while me and C hit it up and then hop in! Ain't no way the cops get here before we out!" Josh replied.

With a reasonable plan, the others waited with Wood while Josh and I went for the car. It only took Josh one strike to blast open the window, but he cut his hand on the glass when he reached inside the car to unlock the door.

"Bro back up!" I said with a whisper. "They can get yo' ass if you bleed in this car!"

"How you know?" he asked.

"Tay told me!" My friends and I had often relied upon Tay's encyclopedic knowledge of mostly useless information. Knowing Tay was one of the smartest kids at school, his word seemed to be enough to persuade Josh to back away and let me finish the job. I grabbed a money clip filled with one-hundred-dollar bills and credit cards, along with a wallet nearby with additional cash.

"Clay you fast as hell, bruh! Shoulda had him go without you Josh!" Wood said when he sped out of the parking lot after Josh and I climbed into the car moments later.

"Bruh, let's split the cash and I'll give you an extra two hunned if you let me keep the credit cards!" Josh said as he reached back and handed me cash.

"Bet," I said, taking the bills and handing him the credit cards.

"Why these people be leaving this kinda money just sittin'?" Jon asked.

"They rich as hell and don't care!" Terrell said. "Ay, Wood, I'm thirsty as hell. Can you pull up in the gas station by the crib?"

"Fuck…they lighting me up!"

We all went into panic mode as Wood informed us that the police were behind him, and we each started reaching down and stuffing everything under the seats.

"This car hot, y'all! I gotta keep goin," Wood said. I kicked myself internally, knowing I should have questioned when I saw him pull up in a vehicle I hadn't seen before.

"Damn, bro! You can't stop or we all going in!" Terrell said in a panic.

I quickly pulled the items from under the seats and stuffed them into my pockets when an idea came to mind. "Just pull over. When the officer get out, gas that shit! That'll give us a head start. When we get to the circle, park and we goin'!" I said to Wood.

"Bet!" he said.

"That's dumb as hell!" Josh said. "Just pull over and let us out one at a time!"

"Hell naw! They just gon' call for backup and arrest us one by one and keep another car behind Wood. Just do what C said!" Terrell said.

Nobody else questioned my idea, and Wood went along with it, agreeing with Terrell that it was the best plan. We waited in silence after Wood stopped the car, and I sat hoping the plan I had suggested would actually help us get home without detection. The only thing I could hear was the accelerated rhythm of my own heartbeat, and the ruminating thoughts that I should have skipped out on the night since I had already made plenty of money from previous nights out. I imagined my brothers finding out what I had been up to and envisioned Jason holding me down while Kemis threw successive punches to my chest.

After what seemed like an eternity, enough time for two additional police cars to arrive, Terrell, Jon, and I watched from the backseat as three officers finally exited their vehicles to approach the car, and subsequently roared in laughter after we saw their expressions when Wood sped off.

"Bruh, he ain't see that shit coming at all!" Terrell laughed.

"Naw! That nigga bout tripped trying to get back to his car! He gon' be pissed, bruh!" Jon yelled.

We were being tossed from side to side as Wood sped through residential streets to keep the distance he had gained from the officers, but we knew our time was limited. He reached an intersection that was only one block from where we needed to be when he saw an officer throwing down what appeared to be handfuls of spikes.

"Ooh he got that shit that make yo' tires flat!" Josh yelled. I took in a deep breath and briefly tucked my eyes down into my palms, unable to watch what happened next out of fear we were nearing either our capture or a dangerous crash.

We all jolted forward as Wood slammed on the brakes, slightly reversed the car, and turned sharply to the left to get around the spikes the officer threw in front of the car. I didn't have the time to process my relief, as the car soon jerked to a halt when we reached the circle, and we all hopped out without so much as a goodbye, running with as much of the evening's spoils as we could safely carry.

It was one of the few times I had gone out without my phone since I was on punishment. I was stooped down outside the apartment looking for a rock to throw at the window when it suddenly creaked open, followed by the escape ladder flopping down.

"Damn, bro. Perfect timing. Rel call you?" I asked once I had made it through the window.

"Bro, y'all was in a stolo?" Tay asked after pushing the window closed.

"Chill, bro. I ain't know 'til he was already getting pulled over. We ain't leave nothing in it though so we good!" I said.

"Did you forget what happened to Day when he was riding in a stolen car?"

"Day *helped* steal that car—the owner saw it and started shooting. I ain't steal no car bro. I just rode in one. It's over now; I made it home and don't nobody know shit but you!" I said.

He looked like he was as disgusted with me as I was with his line of questioning. He was older than me by eleven months but acted in that moment like it was eleven years. For a moment I wished that Daveon was the brother I shared a room with. While he didn't always go along with all my ideas, I felt he wouldn't have been nearly as uptight as Tay about the stolen car.

"Take yo' ass to bed, dude," Tay said before turning out his light and disappearing underneath his blanket and into the darkness of the room. I didn't like the shame of disappointing him, or the fear that he was losing patience with me.

Pastor D also grew impatient when he arrived in my bedroom the next morning to wake me up to go hang out for the day. I slept through my brothers' departures to school and was clinging on to any last bit of sleep I could muster.

"Unc, can't we hang out tomorrow?" I asked, still clutching my pillow with my eyes squeezed shut.

"Let's do both! I'ma tell Kemis you spending the night so I can see why it is you're having so much trouble in the morning! Have you been sneaking on your phone at night?" he asked after his third time removing my blanket from over my body.

"Unc, come on! I ain't even got my phone! And I don't wanna spend the night! You be extra!"

My desire to stay where I was did not keep him and Kemis from packing my bag with three days' worth of clothing along with my homework, while I sat in the bed pouting and trying to explain that I was tired, a rant that fell on deaf ears. The only good that came from being thrown in the car with Pastor D was that he told me he was taking me to breakfast, but it turned south when I realized he was pulling into the parking lot of a hotel my crew and I were in the previous night. I panicked, wondering if he knew what I had done the night before, and wondering what I needed to say to get him to turn the car around.

"Unc…uh…wait, what you doing? I thought we was gon' go to breakfast first? Look, Unc, I'm—"

"Clay, calm down son! This hotel has the best breakfast in the area! You'll love it! Zip up: it's cold out!" he said cheerfully and opened the door to step outside.

I threw my hoodie over my head before getting out of the car, which Pastor D griped at me about and made me take off once we were inside the lobby. I tried to leave it on for as long as I could, especially after noticing a police vehicle outside the lobby doors, and then two uniformed officers who appeared to be speaking with hotel employees in the lobby. My heart sank while I tried to avoid staring in the direction of the officers, hoping they couldn't see my face and somehow know my secret.

"Boy, I told you to take that hoodie off inside!" Pastor D said after we reached the entryway to the restaurant.

While taking my hoodie down, I said several silent prayers that God would keep anyone from recognizing me. I told God that if he kept me from getting caught, I would go to church and get saved, actually listen during the services, pray every day, and I would stop sneaking out to steal. The prayer must have worked, since other than my paranoia about the police being nearby, we had a delicious breakfast with the fluffiest buttered blueberry waffles and savory roasted sweet potatoes I had ever tasted.

We were led through a set of double doors to a private seating area outside of the main dining area that was nested outside, heated with firepits and heating lamps. Even though Pastor D used mealtime to lecture about my behavior, being able to overlook a pond with a relaxing waterfall in the outside air helped me to cope with being talked at. He promised to bring me back if my behavior improved and I had a good report card, and I promised that I would earn a trip back.

The next portion of our day was not as appealing. The relief I had when we left the hotel was short-lived, lasting only until he dragged me to church to fold pamphlets and set up chairs for a conference that was going to be held later that week. I was refused every time I requested to do something more fun or interesting, and scolded every time he caught me off task, which was often.

As if that wasn't annoying enough, he later hauled me to a shelter that was operated by the church where I was forced to help some older ladies with bad perfume set up for a children's Valentine's party. I was forced to blow up pink and white balloons and plaster decorations on the wall, pour red punch from a bowl into small cups, set up games, and sprinkle girly-looking confetti on tabletops. Even worse, when he found out they were short volunteers, Pastor D made me stay for the party to pass out drinks and cake, and to read books to little kids. I worked non-stop for hours until nearly four o'clock, when I became tired, hungry, and mouthy, so much so that Pastor D threatened to bring me out for two more days of service if I didn't stop talking back.

I was rescued from the party and started having fun when an eleven-year-old resident of the shelter named Jackson asked me if I wanted to come to the gym and join in a basketball game. Basketball was the last thing I thought he would ask me about since I hadn't seen a gym around. He approached with a faint smile and was friendlier than most of the kids I was used to being around. But his clothing appeared much more worn than anything BJ had ever teased me about. Even worse, his shoes didn't look like they could survive a casual stroll across the room, let alone a basketball game, as portions of his sock peeked in between holes on the side of his left shoe.

We snuck away and intensely played the same way I did at the basketball court at home, and I found myself back in my happy place and feeling like I was winning the day again. I was the only non-resident in the full-court game, but felt accomplished when everyone wanted to join my team before starting the next game. Unfortunately, our hopes for another game were interrupted when Pastor D told me it was time to get home for dinner.

"Ay, you gon' come back sometime, right? You can ball for real!" Jackson said after I unsuccessfully begged Pastor D for more playing time.

"Uh yeah, bruh! I'ma try to come back," I told him. His countenance changed from hopeful to disappointed, as it seemed he could tell that I wasn't completely confident in my answer. I hoped I could come back and play without having to do the work Pastor D had forced me into.

"Unc, what kinda shelter is that one?" I asked him as we were driving away.

"It's a shelter for displaced single moms and their kids…a lot of the women there were in violent situations and needed to get out but didn't have anywhere to go. Some of them were homeless, or about to be homeless due to job loss. We try to get a lot of the families to come over to the church, but some of them feel too embarrassed to come over for worship. So, we started doing a Sunday evening service here…and I come periodically and do youth and children's worship," he said.

"You knew that Jackson kid?" I asked.

"The one who invited you to basketball and made you think you could sneak off without me noticing?" He looked at me with a smirk on his face before continuing. "Yeah, he's a good kid. Him and his mom and younger siblings had to leave a really bad situation. His mother was worried about him because his grades really went downhill during the transition, but he's turned things around a little bit," he said.

"How long they been there?" I asked, wondering if Jackson was tired of living in a shelter.

"I think it's been around a year or so. His mom has been trying to secure a housing voucher. Once she does that, they'll probably be able to get into a small apartment," he responded.

"His shoes looked like they were like ten years old!"

"They came with nothing but the clothes on their backs. His mother was able to get a minimum wage job, but it's barely enough to get them the basics, let alone buy them all new shoes all the time. The church gives a lot of money in donations but it often goes to school supplies, underwear, toiletries…other basic necessities," he said.

I silently pondered what he said, marveling that Jackson seemed so happy despite having so little, even less than me and my brothers.

"It's something, huh?" he continued. "Makes you realize how much you have to be thankful for. I mean, you and your brothers haven't had it easy. But you've managed to stay out of a shelter. Your small apartment would be like a mansion compared to their living quarters. But for them, living there is better than sleeping in the car, which is what they were doing. Can you imagine having to do your homework after school in the front seat of a car?" he asked.

"I just wouldn't do it. Homework lame anyway," I said.

He softly chuckled and shook his head. "You're fortunate to have a quiet room with a bed to yourself that you can do homework on...or a couch…or even older brothers that can help you if you don't know what to do," said Pastor D.

"Or older brothers that are lame and try to boss you around all the time," I said.

"Or older brothers that love you so much they won't let you run crazy and ruin your life before it even gets started! Your brother is much more tolerant of your antics than I would be," he said.

I knew he wouldn't understand my complaints about my brothers and my living situation, especially after leaving the shelter. Still, something about seeing Jackson made me want to help him. While I never had the best basketball shoes before I started making money, they at least didn't look like they would fall apart while I played the way Jackson's and some of the other kids' shoes looked. I recently purchased a pair that I knew I would have to keep at school to keep my brothers from getting suspicious about my activities, and I considered whether I should bring them home for Jackson.

"Some stuff just ain't fair, Unc," I said.

"Yeah, like what?" he asked.

"Like, how some people don't have anything, and some people have everything," I uttered, thinking of some of the luxury cars my friends and I had stolen from. Some people had so many extra pairs of shoes that they just let them sit in their cars unattended. Others had so much cash they could leave it in their cars for later, while we needed government assistance just to keep enough food to eat.

"That may seem unfair. Or maybe sometimes we place too much value on the wrong things."

16

ONE LAST WORD

The two suspensions that came shortly after the fight were equally petty in my book, but Kemis took them a lot more seriously, probably because they impacted him in an unexpected way. The first one was a zero-day suspension, which meant I was not allowed to return to school until Kemis had a meeting with the principal. The school policy required an automatic suspension if a student reached a certain number of writeups in one month, and my sleepiness and mouthiness caused me to meet that threshold rather quickly, despite having been out of school for a large chunk of the month.

Kemis came to school the same day the suspension was issued and met with the principal and the assistant principal to discuss all the write-ups that caused the suspension. He was upset that he hadn't known about the write-ups. They told him that notifications were mailed home, but he didn't know that I was slipping them out of the mail and throwing them in the dumpster in the back alley. Since I thought that his anger was directed to my teachers for not contacting him on the phone, I mistakenly assumed his mood would be decent once we departed.

In between his bouts of yelling during the car ride home, I tried pleading with him that some of the write-ups were petty. "I mean, c'mon K. Some of those write ups were for getting to class late too many times. That's just stupid," I said, but my words only infuriated him more.

He grit his teeth when he started speaking, "Bro, I don't care if they were for picking your nose too many times! How many times have I told you that if it's against the school rules, don't do it! And not all of them were for being tardy. Some of them were for leaving class early, skipping class altogether, and some were for your smart-ass mouth that we've talked about. And why you late to class so daggone much? Most of your classes are on the same hallway!" he yelled.

I didn't have a response that I could offer and keep my life intact. Even though I had largely left the snack store thefts to the others, some of the write-ups were attributable to times in the store and to my hallway transactions.

Kemis took my phone and ordered me to my room after a tumultuous ride, and I sat wondering if I should use my newfound cash to purchase a phone from Flip. Although I was supposed to be doing homework while confined to my room, I instead dozed off, awakened only by Daveon. who had come in the room to start grilling me.

"You better get up 'fore K find you in here sleeping and whoop yo' ass! Why you acting bad at school?" he asked. It was hard to take him seriously when I was certain he still held the record for the most suspensions and detentions in the whole house, even though he hadn't been suspended or sent to detention since the previous school year.

"Day, these teachers be on some other stuff. They just write me up for any little thing now," I said.

"That's 'cause you been acting up fuh so long. You think if Tay get to class late, his teachers say anything?" he asked.

"No, they probably apologize to him for starting without him," I cracked.

"Bro, you need to chill or K gon' kick yo' ass! You know his boss told him if he keep leaving work early they gon' suspend him! If he lose his job then what we gon' do bro?" he asked.

"I don't be trying to get in trouble. Sometimes I just end up in the wrong place at the wrong time," I said.

"Or with the wrong people," he said. He was pissed at my friends ever since the mall incident that Jason told him about, and they both blamed them for my problems at school.

Pastor D cracked opened the door to my room after a few light taps. "Hey fellas," he said.

"Sup Unc," Day said as he got up to leave.

"Day, don't go anywhere; I need to see you before I go," Pastor D said to Daveon before turning to me. "I feel like we keep having the same talk over and over again, Clay. And I know for a fact your brother feels that way. His patience is wearing a little thin with you."

I didn't respond. I thought my teachers and principal had been petty, but I knew I couldn't tell him that. I knew there was nothing I could say that would get him on my side. If I told him the truth, he'd only respond in Bible scriptures.

"You're usually not this quiet. What's on your mind?" he asked.

"I'ma be good," I muttered. It was all I could come up with and figured it was what he wanted to hear.

"Well, don't do better for me. You should do it for you and for God," he said.

I wondered if he ever had a conversation without talking about God. I didn't want any more God talk. I remembered all those people who had spoken at Granny's funeral saying God brought her home to Him, and it had made me angry. I didn't know why God felt He needed her more than we did. I didn't understand why He didn't know how badly losing her would rip our hearts to shreds.

"Do you want to talk about it?" he asked me, but I wasn't interested. I was frustrated with the fact that they seemed so concerned about what the teachers thought, but hardly seemed to care how I felt about it. I shook my head before reclining onto my bed.

"I feel strongly that something is going on with you Clay…something much deeper than your behavior at school. You can always come to me, regardless of what it is. But if it's something bad, it's always better to let the Lord lead you out of it before he exposes it," he continued. "Do you remember that weekend when Kemis and Jason went to visit Duke, and you three spent the weekend with me?" he asked.

"Yeah…" I said, wondering what he was getting at.

"Remember how Tay decided to give his heart to the Lord, and you said that you weren't ready because you weren't good like Tay? You remember that?"

I remembered it clearly, but tried to pretend I only vaguely recalled it. "Uh, I think so."

"God's not after just the good ones, Clay. We all need him. Sick people need a doctor. Broke people need a lender. Hungry people need food. Thirsty people need water. Sinners need forgiveness…from God. All of us do…and it doesn't matter what you've done."

I kept my eyes from meeting his as I nervously listened while he grabbed my hand and started praying something about me being free and "loosed from the enemy." He prayed as though he knew exactly what I had been doing, and I restrained myself from offering a tearful confession by biting my lips together. Before he left, he relayed that Kemis said I was grounded to my room and that I needed to complete my homework.

Watching him close the door sent my brain and body into a mild panic. My breathing was heavy and so was my heart after considering all of Pastor D's words, and the idea of being trapped inside my room only intensified my feelings. I was desperate to be outside in fresh, cooler air, even if just for a few minutes, and I became anxious to sneak out and seek peace at the basketball court.

I slowly opened my door to peek into the hallway just to see if I could hear where Kemis was, right as Pastor D came out of Daveon's room.

"I know you not thinking about going down to that basketball court after your brother said you grounded, young man!" His voice startled me.

"Naw, uh, I was, I needed to pee!" I tried to sound convincing and inched toward the bathroom where I knew I'd have to somehow force liquid to exit my body. I closed the door behind me and stayed until he walked down the steps, and I waited until after he went home to sneak out.

Kemis woke me up early the next morning, which I thought was to talk to me about not completing my homework the night before. Instead, it was to remind me that I was to follow every single rule at school, since any more write-ups for the month would result in another automatic suspension. He added a few threats of violence if I didn't comply, to which I responded with my standard "whatever" under my breath.

I went the next few days being careful not to use profanity around any teachers and arriving to my classes on time, but couldn't resist spectating later on that week when Terrell told me about a fight that would be going down at the beginning of fourth period. The others in my crew planned to skip class so they wouldn't have to miss the fight, but I decided not to skip, knowing I was dead with one more write-up. I decided instead to slip into class after the fight, unwilling to miss an event that would likely be discussed for weeks and maybe years to come.

We loitered at one of our hiding spots in the back of the school until the time came to watch the fight, which did not disappoint. There was a big crowd, some of whom were sure to capture the brawl on video, egging on the two seventh grade girls that fought. My boys and I cracked jokes about who was winning, with Josh yelling at the girls to rip each other's shirts. We saw shirts and hair come off just before security disappointingly swarmed the crowd, prompting the four of us to run before we ended up getting busted along with the slow runners by the security guards.

Jon and I snuck into the teacher's lounge on the way back inside to buy a soda and snack from the vending machine. It was something only the kids who kept extra money were able to do, and now that my friends and I had money and regularly needed caffeine and sugar to stay awake for our classes, we often stopped in the lounge to take advantage of having better drink and snack selections. Joining a group of kids with purchased snacks from the teacher's lounge felt like a badge only the bold and prosperous could wear, and I proudly wore it whenever I had the opportunity.

I had just popped open my soda when I opened the door to enter class and looked over to see the soda had fizzed out and spilled all over the floor, causing everyone in the room to stare at me and my soda. My teacher was at the chalkboard in the middle of the lesson, and apparently was not in the mood for soda fizz.

"Don't even come in my classroom, Clay. Just go straight to the principal's office. I'm not accepting you this late. Tell him the write-up will be there shortly," she said.

My stomach dropped as she said the words "write-up." I froze as they echoed between my ears, and I knew I would have to talk her out of it by making outer worldly promises to behave better.

"Miss Roberts, don't write me up! You let people come in here late all the time! And I didn't mean to spill this—I'ma wipe it up. It must've gotten shaken up when I was running—"

"Running to class knowing you were late since you got held up at that fight where a lot of other students were that came in late as well," she said, cutting me off.

I hadn't known at the time that there had been kids already seated in class that had also arrived in late from watching the fight. I had come even later than them, likely because they didn't stop for soda.

"Miss Roberts—"

"Goodbye Clay!" she responded.

"Yo, you be doing too much!" I said.

"Leave now or I'm calling security!" she said.

I couldn't leave without getting in the last word. "You on that petty bullshit today," I announced as I walked out, almost wishing I could suck the words back into my mouth.

I found a seat in the vestibule outside of the principal's office before going in so I could finish my soda, as though I was enjoying the last tasty beverage I would ever consume. I knew that I had secured another suspension, guaranteeing the likelihood that Kemis would once again treat me like a prisoner.

Mr. Mack bid me into his office when I finally arrived, asking me what brought me in.

"I got to class late," I told him in a defeated tone as I walked past the two girls that had been fighting, both seated in opposite sides of the room, looking like they were dreading the arrival of their parents.

I strolled in and sat down across from his desk, where he started talking to me about the most recent suspension and write-ups. He stood and closed the door before returning to his seat, and stared curiously at his screen before he lowered his glasses and peered at me over the frames.

"So apparently Miss Roberts wrote you up for being twenty-five minutes late to class! She said she believes you were at the fight. After she sent you to my office, you told her she was on, and I quote, 'petty bullshit!'" he replied.

He read, put his glasses back on, and subsequently lowered them again to look at me as if he was awaiting a response.

"You know I'm going to have to suspend you for this," he continued. "This really disappoints me."

I was shocked that he was disappointed since I had assumed that he always labeled me a failure anyway, but he was one of the few people at school that didn't discuss the bleakness of my future. He seemed to have at least partially entertained the idea that I had a chance to live a decent life. I wondered if he had evicted that idea from his psyche now that I had proven I would never be as well-behaved as my brother Tay.

"I really thought this last suspension would motivate you to get back on the right track. I don't want to send you home, but you know I can't allow you to continue in your same behavior, and I definitely can't allow you to speak to teachers in that manner," he said. He shook his head and peered around the room, seeming unsure of how to proceed. "You can sit out there while I type this up. I'll send your teachers messages to gather your work, and I'll write you a pass for your classes"

"How long am I suspended for?" I asked.

"I'm going to send you home for one full day, and then you will do one day of in-school suspension."

I hated sitting at in-school suspension more than sitting on the front row at church, but I figured it could be better than being on punishment with Pastor D or home with Kemis and being forced to complete one of his chore lists. Either way, I wasn't trying to see my brother to tell him what happened, but soon realized I wouldn't have to. When he wrote my pass, Mr. Mack called Kemis to tell him what happened, and told him they needed to have a conference later that afternoon.

I wasn't sure what time my death was coming that night since we were all supposed to go to Jason's basketball game, but since I knew it was impending, it was all I could think about during my last two periods. I ran into Jon after school and told him everything that had transpired, and how I knew my brother wouldn't receive the news of my suspension very well.

"Yo, I got something for you; come with me real quick," he said. I followed him, not knowing if I should go anywhere else with him that day. When we arrived at his locker, he reached in and handed me a pack of Alka-Seltzer tablets.

"What's this?" I asked, unsure why he was handing me medicine for getting suspended from school.

"Ay look, if you put these in your mouth when you 'bout to get a whoopin, you gon' start foamin at the mouth, and then he'll stop. I did it with my mama one time, and she got so scared she stopped and got me some water," he laughed. I looked at him like he was insane, trying to figure out if he was joking or serious. "Dude, I'm for real," he said. "Keep it in your pocket."

"You crazy man," I said.

"You coming out later? You know we hitting up some stuff tonight!" he exclaimed.

"Doubt it, bruh. Jay gotta game and K prolly gon' make me stay wit' Unc. I'll holla at you later," I said.

17

LESS MONEY, MORE PROBLEMS

I was surprised to see Pastor D waiting in the front room on the couch once Tay and I walked inside. He stood and told Tay and Daveon to grab their things so he could take them to do homework, get dinner, and meet us at the game.

"I heard you had a rough day," Pastor D said.

"Kinda," I said with a shoulder shrug, not really wanting to go into detail about the dumb things I had done that day.

"Did you make good choices?" he asked in a low voice. All I could do was look around the room and down at the floor, knowing I didn't have a good answer. "Actions have consequences, Clay. And you've got to learn to control your behavior and especially that tongue," he said.

I already knew what I needed to do as far as my mouth was concerned, I just hadn't quite figured out how to do it and was hating his reminder in that moment.

"We'll see y'all later," Pastor D called out as he left with Tay and Daveon. I was jealous that they were headed out to have fun while I was forced to stay home with the face of hell. Kemis locked the door behind them and looked over at me.

"Go head to yo' room. I'll be up there in a minute," he said grimly. I could tell by his expression that he didn't have any plans for me that I would enjoy.

I threw down my backpack and sprawled out on the bed to gather my thoughts once I was upstairs but had little time to do so. Within seconds my brother was stomping up the steps, and I hadn't even had time to grab extra underwear. I remembered the Alka Seltzer in my pocket and scrambled to unwrap it and throw it in my mouth right before my brother was hovering in the doorway with a belt tightly clenched in his hand.

"Stand up," he ordered as he advanced toward me. He yanked me off the bed when I didn't stand and began to strike me so hard that I knew I had to try whatever it took. I yelled out and looked at him with my mouth open and felt foam and fizz coming out the sides of my mouth. He stopped hitting me and looked panicked like he was about to call an ambulance or administer CPR, but his glance softened within a few moments.

"Boy, please, I did that when I was your age too," he said, and immediately resumed swinging while I tried to pull away from him.

It burned worse than the burning on my tongue from the stupid Alka Seltzer, and I hated that he was so strong, rendering my efforts to block or get away completely meaningless. All I could do was wiggle and jump and jolt as wildly as possible, and cry after pretending for as long as I could that it didn't hurt.

He walked out of the room without saying any words while I remained on the floor with only my sniffles, my burning tongue, and my regrets. I wanted to turn on the PlayStation to get my mind off of everything, but I didn't want Kemis to hear and come back upstairs. Instead, I tiptoed out the house and down the street to the basketball court, with a plan to drown out my sorrows over a cold game of street ball.

It had been one of those days that was cold enough to weed out the serious ballers from the undedicated at the basketball court. To be outside comfortably would have required a heavy coat, a known barrier to the perfect jump shot. There were a few guys at one end of the court already in a game, and I shot around by myself on the opposite side, undesirous of any interaction. I dribbled as though a fierce defender guarded me and shot turnaround jumpers for my invisible crowd that cheered me on from non-existent bleachers. I ignored the fact that my fingers could barely bend or flex after a while due to the cold, and at points pounded the ball down with a closed fist in efforts to preserve warmth and feeling in my hands.

"Let's go, dude!" My brother suddenly called with his head hanging impatiently outside the driver's side window of his truck. I had already known it was Kemis when I heard an engine grinding near the fence, and I attempted one last basket in hopes that it would take the edge off his anger with me for sneaking out.

I grabbed my ball and sulked over, hoping that at least if I was about to be hit again, it wouldn't be on the parking lot for everyone to watch. To my surprise, he didn't speak to me when I got into my seat, but his facial expression bore all of his thoughts and feelings about my venture out. He was breathing hard enough for me to sense his disturbance in my own lungs. He placed his hand on the gear shift as though he was about to reverse, but then took it off and sat back in his seat, staring off like he wasn't sure what to say to me.

"What happened today, man? And don't tell me no BS story cause I ain't got time for it," he said.

It seemed typical of him, Granny, and every other adult I knew to ask questions after already whooping my tail, and I found myself feeling annoyed. I shrugged my shoulders and continued staring out the window.

"Nah bro, that ain't gon' work," he said, sounding ready to come at me again. I really hoped he hadn't planned to skip out on Jason's game, as I loathed the thought of being subjected to answering uncomfortable questions all night long.

"My teachers come after me over little shit. Then you beat my ass all because I got to class late and spilled a fucking soda. You just like them!" I said.

He sighed while turning his head out of the opposite window from me. "Watch your mouth, lil' bro," he said in a voice much calmer than I expected. "I lost my job today. All because I needed an hour off to talk to your principal. I knew it would happen. They told me if I left early again I'd be fired. I had to leave. They fired me. Petty as hell. But guess what—sometimes one more fuckup can screw you up for good! That's me! That's us!"

I initially assumed he was exaggerating but looked up and saw the uncertainty in his expression, signaling that he was truly worried about his job status.

"When the other manager come back from vacation," he continued, "I'ma try to get back on, but that's gonna be almost a week. I'ma have to take some extra Uber shifts to try to get some extra cash this week! I can't afford to lose hours and miss out on money that we desperately need, bro—Tay is scheduled to take another test to see if he can get into one of the top high schools in the area. They are offering a scholarship, but it doesn't cover everything. You know Jason always needs stuff for basketball. Y'all need stuff for school…AAU is gon' cost money. Day has a pricey school trip coming up. But if I'm losing money and we're not even making ends meet now, I definitely won't be able to afford any extra expenses. Sometimes, you gotta think about how your actions impact the rest of us." He sighed and shook his head before finally putting the car in reverse. "Look, we'll talk more about this later. We gotta get to this game," Kemis said.

I reflected on my brother's words more than I let on. While I sat pretending as though his words had no impact, I actually felt awful that I was the cause of his unemployment and our worsening financial status. Seeing him look so stressed hurt way worse than when he had hit me earlier, and I wondered if I should go out for extra work with my crew to help him pay bills. At the same time, I knew him, and I knew he wouldn't accept cash from me without questioning where it came from.

I spent some of the time at Jason's game wondering how to fix what I had done. I thought about Jackson from the shelter and wondered if we would become his neighbors once Kemis would no longer be able to pay rent. I wished I hadn't made poor choices at school and had focused more on securing money to help my brother, which I did when I was able to sneak out of the gym a few times.

18

POLICE PRESENCE

"I heard you got suspended again…you aight?" Jason asked me when we reached his car after his game. He told me he wanted me to ride home with him, which meant I had to wait forever after the game was over since there were a lot of people wanting to speak with him, interview him, take selfies, or even request an autograph. It was a tedious wait for someone as tired as I had been, who had once again used game time to car clot on one of the residential streets across from the school.

I looked away and nodded my head in response to his question, not wanting to delve deeply into a discussion surrounding my bad behavior or our impending homelessness.

"K musta whooped yo' tail 'cause you seem mad. What you do at school to get suspended again?" he asked.

"All I did was get to class late 'cause I watched a fight, and they gon' make a big deal outta that shit," I told him.

"That part was lame, but didn't you cuss at your teacher again?" he asked.

I sighed. "Bro, she was extra lame! Talmbout she gon' call security on me…over a fucking tardy and a soda. I can't stand that lady. I can't stand school period."

"Well, you not old enough to stop going. And you definitely ain't old enough to be cussing out no grown ass teachers. You probably need to chill on all the fighting too bro. You don't want to end up like Day and have to go to summer school every year because of your grades or because you missed so much school with your suspensions. Trust me, you'll have way more fun in AAU than in summer school," he said.

"We ain't got money for AAU," I said, reflecting on Kemis' job loss.

"Unc paid for mine, bro—every time, and he said he would pay for yours and Day's too. But prolly not if you keep acting up…and why you keep sleeping in your classes?" he asked.

I immediately felt tense all over, wondering if he was asking because of something he had heard. I shrugged my shoulders and looked straight ahead, hoping he didn't suspect that I was staying up and sneaking around at night.

"Lil' bro, you know I be trying to talk K down when he be on you, but you don't be helping when you keep acting up!" Jason pulled the car into a parking spot in front of the gas station a block away from our apartment complex. "Come on, let's get a drink."

I didn't want to go inside since I knew my friends and I regularly stole from the gas station shop, and I didn't want to risk someone recognizing me. But he wouldn't let me wait in the car and told me he would buy me something, unaware that I had a pocket full of cash and credit cards from my evening adventures.

"Jason, I hate I missed the game, man! I heard you balled out though!" a voice called out when we walked through the door.

One of the managers at the counter knew Jason by name, as did most people who worked at the station, and always chatted him up after home games. Jason smiled and approached the counter to talk about the game and told him about his senior night game that was coming up. I hung back near the fountain drinks to start filling my cup with different sodas while waiting for Jason to join me.

Our journey quickly turned from casually choosing drinks to hugging the floor for safety when we were startled by what sounded like rapid explosions coming from the parking lot in front of the store.

"Bro get down!" Jason yelled as he jumped and tackled me to the ground and swarmed over my body as the popping sounds drew closer, but not loud enough to drown out the sounds of tires outside screeching, followed by the shattering of the storefront glass door crashing in pieces to the floor.

"Stay down!" he said while I was still sprawled out with my hands palmed down on a soda-stained floor. I rested my forehead on the backs of my hands and whispered a quick prayer that we wouldn't die. Other patrons in the store started slowly scrambling, and Jason slightly lifted the top of his body off of mine to glance around once the popping sounds drifted away.

After a voice from behind the counter yelled out to ask if everyone was okay, Jason slowly stood up with his hands on top of his head while I stared blankly at the stack of unused cups, unsure if I wanted a refill since I had knocked my first one over when Jason shuffled us both to the floor. Within a few minutes we heard sirens and the sounds of walkie talkies as multiple police officers had arrived on scene, triggering an even greater agitation than I had felt when we were on the floor evading bullets. I asked Jason if we could leave when the police requested that everyone stay inside until they had gotten their name, number, and a brief statement.

"Bro, just chill. It shouldn't take long," he started before his phone began to buzz. He looked at it and shook his head. "K gonna kill me for not going straight home like he said," he griped before answering his phone. "K, I'm sorry."

Kemis' panicked voice was too loud to be contained by the earpiece in Jason's phone. He explained how they had been headed home from the store and were driving by the gas station when he saw the large police presence and Jason's car in the center of it. The police wouldn't let him onto the lot when he tried to come in and check on Jason and me.

"K, we fine, bro…I think there was a shoot-out in the lot, but we were inside when it happened." I was relieved he didn't tell him about the shots through the storefront door. "The police want a quick statement from us," he said as one of the officers walked up. "Look, we're about to talk to an officer. I promise we'll leave as soon as we're done. No—K, you don't need to come up here. Clay is fine, bro! Okay, aight."

None of us really trusted the police, but especially not after a neighborhood teenager was shot by an officer just a few streets over from our house. We didn't know all the details, but we knew he was black, he didn't have a gun, and a white cop killed him, leaving his lifeless body in the street for hours afterwards.

Within minutes of the shooting, one of Jason's friends told him about it, and the four of us walked to the scene to join hundreds of onlookers, since Kemis was gone to one of his classes, and Granny had been out running errands. We viewed the slain body lying in the street, and the crowd that was gathering was getting larger by the minute and more impatient with the police officers who paced around talking amongst themselves as if unsure of what to do next instead of covering the teen's body.

The case sparked national and international attention, and we marveled at news stories covering protests around town as well as riots that were near our apartment complex. On a few occasions, Jason and Daveon snuck out to the protests at the police station, but Kemis pounded them both when he found out, afraid they would get caught up in a violent encounter.

We were all angry a few months later when a white prosecutor announced on live television that the killer would not be charged, making it seem like the kid deserved to get shot. We knew some people, mostly white people, said that had he cooperated he'd still be alive, but black people from our neighborhood knew better.

We had witnessed the police harass too many innocent people, including Kemis and Jason, who often got pulled over for no reason. One time he took Jason with him to visit his girlfriend, who lived in a majority white neighborhood, and the police pulled up on them with guns drawn, ordering them to get out and on the ground.

Kemis constantly reminded us to always behave like we were in the presence of a bad officer during every police encounter. We tried to do so that night at the gas station, but it became increasingly difficult after an officer started by asking us basic information, but then transitioned into questioning us regarding our reasoning for being in the area. He asked where we had come from, where we were headed, if we had been in any fights, and who we'd been fighting with. He repeatedly asked why we ran inside the store, even after Jason told him we were already inside when everything happened. He started questioning Jason as if he somehow knew the people who were in the lot shooting or was in some way involved.

Having become impatient with the questions, I piped up after the officer asked if he could search us for weapons, particularly since I did not see anyone else getting searched. "What the hell you trying to search us for?" I asked irritably. "You act like *we* did some shit!"

"Shhh. Clay! Listen, I'm sorry about my brother, Officer. We weren't involved, and we don't have nothing on us! We need to get outta—"

The store manager who knew Jason walked up and interrupted to talk to the officer for a few moments, which changed the trajectory of the conversation.

"You boys be safe getting home. Please drive out the back of the lot since the front will be blocked," the officer said with a sudden change in tone after turning his attention back to Jason and me. I could tell Jason wanted to go off on him but held back. Had it been Daveon, we would've been in in handcuffs and getting tased, I thought to myself.

19

WE GON' BE ALRIGHT…I HOPE

Kemis seemed more upset than we were when we arrived back home. He huddled in the cold on the front stoop, waiting for us with a coat and a blanket covering him, and jumped up when we pulled into a nearby parking space. He grabbed us both and pulled us into him once we reached the porch until Jason reassured him repeatedly that we were okay.

"K why you wait in the cold like that bro? I told you we aight!" Jason said once we were inside.

We turned toward the front door after hearing the lock being maneuvered, followed by Kory entering inside. Despite his words that they weren't planning to date each other, the two had become close friends, and he had given her a spare key to the apartment for emergencies.

"Hey babe," she said to Kemis after scrambling through the door. Afterwards she looked over at Jason and me. "Are you boys okay?"

"We good! The screaming and the glass shattering were worse than the gunshots—no one got hit," Jason said.

The three of them turned to me as though they wanted to hear my thoughts on what had happened.

"I'm cool," was all I wanted to offer. I was a little shaken up, but the day had been too eventful to be able to break down for them how I was feeling.

Although I drifted off to my room to get ready for bed before they finished talking, I knew I was preparing for another sleepless night. My brain was bouncing around and my body was too tired to bounce with it, and I found myself playing on Tay's phone late into the night, to keep me company and to keep my mind off of the day's events. I eventually fell into a short-lived sleep, as I was jolted up in the middle of the night from the sounds of glass shattering and bullets firing. I was trapped on the floor with Jason on top of me, feeling as though death had finally captured me on the gas station floor. I had been close to death before, but this time the closeness felt disturbing enough to get up and scream at death, telling it to leave me alone.

I looked over to Tay's bed to see that he was stiffly nested underneath his blanket, making me unsure if I had screamed out loud or not. After limping over to the bathroom sink to rinse the sweat from my face, I crept to Jason's room and saw that he was sitting up in bed with his back against the wall, with the light from his phone illuminating his face in the dark room.

"You can't sleep either?" he asked in a low voice as he moved over and made room for me. I shook my head and got into bed next to him, pressing the back of my head on a pillow he wasn't using.

"Jay, why you gotta leave for college? It's D-one schools here! We could come to all your games, and you could be home on the weekends and hang out," I said. They had recently been talking more about his upcoming signing day for school, and it upset me every time he talked about it. In the midst of that, one night he and Kemis had gotten into an early morning shouting match over Jason's missed curfew, and Jason angrily reminded us all that he would be gone in a few months.

"You gon' miss me, lil' chicken nugget?" he asked. He was smiling, but I wasn't in the mood to make light of it all. The way he had looked out for me at the gas station reminded me that I couldn't afford to lose him to a basketball program across the country. "Look. If I tell you this, you can't tell anyone because I don't want the word out yet. I won't be that far away. I'll be able to come home some weekends when the season is out. I can't take Granny's car with me, but I already know some people at a school nearby that I can ride home with sometimes. I'll be home all the holidays we don't have games or practice. Plus, y'all will be able to come spend the weekend and see me play sometimes. Before the season starts, I'll see if y'all can come down on the Greyhound for one of the football games. K already said Day could go. But I know he not letting you come if you keep clowning like you been doing," he said.

"I'm done clowning," I said, reflecting on how clowning had defeated me that day.

"Yeah, you said that like three suspensions ago. But you better be done. I'll find a way home and kick your little ass if I have to, I promise."

"Don't be extra like K," I said.

"Sometimes he drives me crazy too, and sometimes he takes shit way too far. But you know that dude would do anything for us. He's doing more than what our parents ever tried to do," he said.

Even though I knew he was right, I didn't like reflecting on our parents. I didn't feel like I had a relationship with Ma and didn't really care to be around her, but sometimes I wished we could have a normal household the way some of our friends had.

I often wondered what it would be like to grow up as a child of Pastor D. I probably wouldn't like it because he was so strict, but at least he provided financially for his family, I thought. I enjoyed talking to him when I wasn't in trouble, which wasn't often. I liked when we would go shop, or go to a basketball game, or go to his house for dinner.

Kemis had watched his own dad get gunned down. He was nine or ten at the time, and had to reach over his dad's body to grab his phone and call police. He told us he had never been the same since that day, but that losing his dad had motivated him to be present for the rest of us. My other brothers never mentioned their dads, other than Tay, who would occasionally receive a letter that he would quickly skim before crumpling up and tossing it in the trash.

Nobody would ever talk about my dad, including Granny, who I prayed would one day give me some answers about him. I had reached the age where I realized that everyone intentionally changed the subject if I mentioned it, especially Kemis.

"How come we know about everyone's dad but mine?" I asked, hoping Jason would continue being open and transparent.

"I'ma keep it real Clay. I remember your dad when I was little. This was back at the old house, and Granny didn't like us around him, and Kemis would cry when he came around. One time I heard Aunt Bebe tell someone that K ran him off. But that's one thing K don't like to talk about, so maybe it's true," Jason said.

For years I had envisioned my reunion with my dad. He would tell me he had no idea that Ma had given birth to a baby, and he'd be so shocked that I looked just like him. He'd be rich and introduce me to a bunch of rich family members, and every other weekend I would go hang with my rich dad who I could talk to about all my problems. My bedroom would be mine alone, with my own television and games. I'd have my own iPad, laptop, and whatever else I needed, and I'd have enough money to give to my brothers. I wondered when…if…he was coming back, and why Kemis would deprive me of a dad just because he no longer had one.

"One day I'ma take care of you, baby bro. They'll wish they never left us," he said.

20

MORE WORK, NO PLAY

Pastor D came by to pick me up the next morning to spend the day with him, and I spent the morning at his kitchen table where he made me draft a two-page apology letter to my teacher for the way I had spoken to her. I didn't know how to fill two whole pages with an apology, so most of the time was spent daydreaming since he wouldn't let me watch television or YouTube or anything with a screen. When I protested, he offered to put on church music while I worked, and I told him I would rather work in silence than listen to lame music.

It took me forever to write one page, and I rewarded myself by going into the backyard to practice free throws. He apparently didn't think I had earned the reward when he found out I was no longer at the table.

"Clay Lands, get your narrow behind over here right now!" Uncle D walked onto the deck through the door from the kitchen to call me over. I bowled the basketball into the grass and walked toward him while he stood with his hands on his waist ready to confront me. "I realize that at home you run off and play basketball before doing what you're supposed to, but that doesn't work here. Get inside and do what I told you!"

"I wrote a page! I was just taking a break!" I said.

"I have nothing against a snack break or a stretch break, but a basketball break is out of the question. Especially since yours usually last two and three hours. Have a seat," he said as he opened the door to reenter the kitchen.

"Ain't nuthin' else to say in the letter. I said sorry and everything else I could say!" I told him in hopes we could pretend the assignment was completed.

"Well, Clay, one thing you're not exactly known for is being at a loss for words—ever. So do like you do any other time and say something. Just make sure it's respectful. But you aren't getting out of this, and I wish you would hurry because I'm getting hungry, and I wanted us to go to lunch."

I angrily plopped down into my seat at the table and crafted enough gibberish to satisfactorily fill out another page so we could leave for a late lunch. He did most of the talking since I was mad with him about the morning assignment, and even more mad after he told me that my afternoon would be spent copying the dictionary, again with no television or phone. I couldn't believe I had to sit where I could see a basketball hoop right outside the door and not even use it.

When we arrived back home, he retrieved the dictionary to show me which page to copy and joined me at the table. I could tell he was about to initiate another lame talk.

"Clay, I want you to know something. I was about to come over last night, but Kemis told me you and Jay seemed fine after what happened. Hearing about the two of you being so close to gunfire really bothered me. It reminded me that tomorrow is not always promised for us, or the ones we love…even the young ones we love. I know you're only twelve years old, but you're still old enough to repent, and give your heart to Jesus. He calls all people of all ages to him. You know he loves you," he said.

"No. I don't," I told him, only partially meaning it. I mainly said it out of annoyance with him, but somewhat because I didn't completely understand why people always said things like "God loves you" when it was impossible to feel his love. It wasn't like he could drop me a hug or some money.

"He definitely does. You know how your brother told you that if you got in trouble at school again, you'd be in trouble with him? Well, God has kinda done the same with us. The Bible tells us that the wages of sin is death. But he sent Jesus to take those sins, and die with those sins, and then God raised him from the dead. And since Jesus already did the hard work for us, and took our punishment for us, all we have to do is believe on him to receive eternal life with him," he said.

"If God loves everyone, how come some people live well and some people struggle? Why he give us a mom that was on drugs? Or why did he let Granny die when my brothers prayed that she would stay alive?" I asked without making eye contact.

He sighed before answering. "Clay, I'm not going to pretend to know all the hard answers. There are a lot of broken people out there having kids, and they don't even realize that they are causing brokenness in their babies. Your parents haven't been there for you, and it's a complete shame. But God is a healer, and he's the only one that can take your pain away. He is faithful to provide, and he rewards those that seek Him, and I really pray that you would find that out for yourself. God can reveal Himself to you. I can lead you in prayer right now. You can accept Jesus, and accept the work he did, and let God handle the rest."

Part of me really did want that prayer, because the things he said sounded like things I needed and wanted. But there was still another part that wanted nothing to do with it, and talking about it made that other part rise up in anger. "No thanks. But if I finish this dictionary thing, can I at least go outside since you won't let me watch anything?" I asked.

He sighed and looked down. "Yes, but only if you answer this question," he said.

"Oh God," I grumbled.

"Don't use the Lord's name in vain in this house…Why is it at home that when you're supposed to do your homework, you sneak off to that basketball court instead of doing what you're told?" he asked.

He looked at me like he was truly interested in my answer. I smiled and put my head down, scratching my head. I wasn't sure how honest I could be on the topic, thinking my answer would get me into trouble no matter what I said. At the same time, the question felt lame considering that some of my friends never did homework, and didn't get nearly as much pushback about it as I did.

"Would you get mad about that if I lived here?" I asked, trying to avoid an answer.

"That would not be tolerated here. And you know you're not supposed to do it, so why do you do it?" he asked.

I shrugged my shoulders and looked up at him.

"I want more than a shoulder shrug," he said, not taking his eyes off me.

"Homework is boring, basketball isn't," I said.

"So basically, you don't like doing homework, so you go and do what you want to do."

"See, I knew you would say that—that's why I ain't wanna answer," I said.

"Well, if it's something different than that, just tell me. Your brother thinks you run to basketball when you're feeling stressed and overwhelmed, which is why he doesn't always go in on you when you sneak off. I, on the other hand, wonder if you're just being defiant. So, help me out. Which one of us is right?"

I still didn't want to answer, but I also wanted to get the conversation over with. "If I answer, can we stop talking about it?" I asked.

"Okay, as you wish," he said as he placed his elbows on the table and crossed his forearms while he stared at me, awaiting my answer.

"Basketball gets my mind off things, and it's the only thing I'm good at. Homework is boring and doesn't get my mind off things. And I'm dumb when it comes to school…I'm not smart like Tay and Kemis. And doing homework ain't gonna make my teachers stop hating me."

With that, he slowly nodded his head and stood up from the table, starting his stroll towards the stairs. "You know where to find the drinks and snacks if you need them. When you're here, this is your home, so be comfortable. Just make sure you finish your work before you go and get your mind off things so you don't find yourself in trouble with me." He paused near the countertop before leaving the room and told me one last thing. "I wish you could see yourself the way God sees you. If you did, you would speak more highly of yourself," he said, leaving me to wonder what it was that God saw that I didn't. Clearly, my friends, teachers, and principal didn't see it either.

21

CLOSE CALLS

I had told the crew that I needed to limit our outings to Friday and Saturday nights to avoid falling asleep in school, but they insisted that more people were out on the weekends, and we would be more likely to get caught. Either way, they humored me that following Saturday night, when we circled back to another apartment complex parking lot near one of the lots where we always left satisfied. Wood drove around the lot to make sure he didn't see anyone before finding the perfect spot to let us out of the car.

"Don't stop here, bruh! It's right under that streetlight," I said.

"That light dim as hell, dude. Can't nobody see yo' black ass noway," Jon laughed, prompting laughter from the rest of the crew.

"Fuck y'all niggas," I said, only partially in jest.

We soon spread out and made our way around the lot, checking to see which cars were unlocked, pulling on door handles, and forcing our way into the ones we thought would be worth it. I quickly hopped in and out of a few cars before landing in a fourth where I rummaged through and found enough to make up for the ones where I turned up empty. There was a wallet with only a small sum of cash but plenty of credit cards. Inside the center console was a loaded Glock that I quickly threw into my bag. Underneath that was a bonus find—a three-pack of chocolate candy bars.

Feeling content with my finds, I sat back and peeled the wrapper off one of the candy bars when Josh began talking in a low voice.

"Yo C! Someone coming!"

I looked up and quickly hopped out, leaving the vehicle door ajar, and tiptoed toward the front of the car behind Josh just as we heard a voice call out.

"Hey! What are you all doing over here? Get out of here you fucking thugs!"

We both turned to see a short, stocky, bald, white man in green plaid pajama pants with a black sweatshirt thrown over the top, scowling at us and quickly approaching as though he was about to strike whoever he could reach first.

"Bitch, step back!" Josh shouted. Just as the man rounded the rear of the car we stood near, Josh snatched up the bottom of his hoodie, revealing what appeared to be the butt of a handgun tucked into the top of his pants.

His revelation surprised both myself and the man, whose eyes widened and body stiffened, and his lips and tongue froze in place. His countenance swiftly changed from anger to devastation, and I could feel the fear that was reflected in his expression. I stopped chewing my chocolate bar and looked over at Josh, who stood in a manner that communicated his willingness to do whatever it took to not get caught. My eyes shifted back to our sorrowful trespasser, who quickly changed course, retreating backwards with his hands raised, demonstrating that he wanted no trouble.

Once we were satisfied with the distance between us and him, I signaled for the others to return to the car, where we all filed in and yelled for Wood to floor us to safety. Knowing that the stranger had likely called police to report seeing kids with guns stealing from cars, I prayed and made a deal with God that if we didn't get caught, I would never go out stealing again, but not before confronting Josh during the ride.

"Yo, what the hell was that, bruh? We coulda just ran!" I yelled.

"Whatchu mean? Sumthin' happen?" Terrell asked.

"Nah, dude rolled up on us like he wanted smoke and called us some thugs so I showed him my choppa, that's it! Ain't like I pointed it at him! Bet he watch who he roll up on next time!" Josh said.

"Damn! You know he calling the police!" Jon said.

I was beyond intrigued at Josh being offended by a simple name-call. But since everyone else seemed to find his explanation reasonable, I left it alone. Still, I was much more uncomfortable with being out with them, not knowing what else Josh might end up doing.

I safely made it home that night without detection, and I actually said another prayer where I thanked God for keeping me out of police custody and allowing me to climb back inside my window without Kemis discovering me and ending my life. I was feeling thankful that God had come through for me, although not exactly ready to hold up my end of the bargain I had made.

22

ONE LAST FLIGHT

"**K**, why you get upset every time I ask you about my dad?" I asked.

I knew the question would catch him off guard. I had what had felt like unlimited amounts of time during my punishment to think about what Jason had told me, and had planned how I wanted to approach Kemis, ultimately deciding that the best way would be to make sure he didn't have time to rehearse an answer.

My other brothers were upstairs occupied with video games and sending messages to girls on their phones. Kemis had just returned inside to finish cleaning the kitchen after walking Kory out to her car, who had been over trying to talk to Jason about having a party for his upcoming signing day where he would officially announce the college he was choosing. Kemis looked as though he was ready to turn in for the night as opposed to satisfy my curiosities. I wondered if I had made the right decision to demand an answer or if I should have approached the subject more gradually. But the more he fidgeted, the more agitated I became.

He sighed, looked at his watch, and looked around like he wanted any way out of talking to me. "Bro, you bringing this up so I don't go in on you for sneaking off to the court earlier even though you on punishment?"

"Damn, bro, I did my homework at least! It ain't got nuthin' to do with that! I been wanting to know like my whole life and you won't ever talk about it!" I said, hoping he would move past my sneak-out to the basketball court.

"Listen, I know we haven't talked about this. I promise you we will, but I've had a long day of job searching and delivering packages and driving people around. How about another night?" he asked.

"That's your excuse? A long day? I've had a long ass day too! I just don't—"

"Watch your mouth baby bro. Look, I agree that you have a right to know. I'm just not sure I can talk to you about it right now. And even if I was, I'm not sure that you're ready for it. Let me make a couple of calls tomorrow."

I shook my head, not finding the patience to endure his reasoning for withholding information that was rightfully mine. I walked away and up the steps to my room, where I pondered how badly I wished I was somewhere else, anywhere that didn't remind me of circumstances that I hated. I hated Kemis, I hated everybody, and I just wished it would all go away in exchange for Granny coming back and life feeling at least partially normal again.

I stood with my back against the door, looking into our tiny room that felt too small for my emotions in that moment, and I knew I needed to get out. I glanced over at Tay's phone, which was charging on his bed, and I yanked it from the cord to call Terrell. He seemed surprised to hear my voice.

"Rel, I'm 'bout to dip. You got any weed?" I asked.

"Naw, but we were about to go get some. Come through!" he said.

I quietly put on my shoes and a hoodie, grabbed a fistful of cash from my stash in the closet, hooked up the fire escape ladder, and crawled my way down to freedom. After safely landing, I ran like I was being chased through the apartment complex parking lot and down the sidewalk toward the intersection, not stopping until I got to Terrell's house, which took nearly six minutes. I sat down on the steps in front of his house to catch my breath before knocking in case his grandma was home. Across the street where the sun was setting on a group of girls playing Double Dutch on the sidewalk, a smaller clan of boys stood nearby watching and laughing at the girls. The scene reminded me of my friends and me hanging outside when we were younger, before the days when we became consumed with making money.

"Clay, what you doing here?" Terrell's older sister Kira asked just as loudly as she smacked her gum when she opened the front door to the house, looking at me as though she wanted me escorted from the property. She and her friend stepped out onto the porch behind where I was seated.

"Nuthin'. Where Terrell?" I asked her while trying to mask the fact that I was out of breath.

She turned behind her and opened up the screen door to call for him. "Rel! Clay out here!"

"C, come on! Granny ain't here," Terrell said, leaning out his bedroom window a few feet over from the front door. I paced back to his room that he shared with his older cousin Deandre, whom we called "Mac."

"Yall better not be in there doing nothing crazy just 'cause Granny working tonight," Kira hollered, knowing we were up to no good.

"Getchu some damn business!" Terrell shouted as he shut and locked his bedroom door.

Mac started chuckling and lit up a blunt and took a hit before he passed it to Terrell, who did the same and passed it to me. Within minutes of us puffing and sharing, I was feeling less tense, and we were talking and laughing, cracking jokes over Snapchat with some of Mac's friends, and then laughing at online videos. We scrolled over our social media pages and played video games for hours, until hunger pangs interrupted our amusement.

Mac suggested we walk to McDonald's, which was only about a five-minute trek, but I told him I couldn't risk being out and getting spotted by one of my brothers, who I figured were out looking for me by then. The two of them ultimately agreed to walk and bring back my order.

They came back with food and cash, as they had stumbled upon a hammer and used it to break into cars on the way back home. They were throwing money around and laughing about their spoils while I opened up the wrapper to the smushed Big Mac and cold fries that Terrell had stuffed into his pocket.

I didn't remember whether I finished all my food, or everything we did after I ate, but I groggily woke up discovering that I had fallen asleep on Terrell's bed. The room was mostly dark except for the light from the television, which was still on, and dimly lit streetlights outside that seeped through the partially draped curtain over Mac's bed. Mac was asleep with a game controller nearby, while Terrell was passed out on the floor, tucked in between McDonald's trash and lopsided pillows, snoring loudly with his hands resting on top of his stomach and underneath his shirt.

I sat up feeling plagued by a fierce headache and a slight aura in my vision and wiped my eyes, thinking things would clear a little. My tongue was parched and desperate for a drop of liquid, and my stomach felt rotten, as though I would puke at any moment. My heart raced as quickly as my thoughts, and I was dizzy and panicking that I didn't know what time it was or what day of the week or if I had slept through school. I searched around the room to get some indication of what time it was and saw on Terrell's phone that it was after one o'clock in the morning. I could only think of one thing: Kemis had probably called the police.

I picked up the phone to call Tay, hoping he wouldn't tell everyone where I was. He answered on the first ring with a panic-stricken tone.

"Terrell, what's up. You seen my brother?" Tay asked.

"Tay, it's me," I whispered.

"Bro, where—" he stopped for a second and then lowered his voice into a whisper. "Where the fuck are you? Unc been over here all night! Kemis been out with Kyle searching for you and so was Jay and Day. They was about to call the police!"

Kemis often called his best friend Kyle to help him keep track of us, but Kyle had a similar temperament to Kemis when it came to us getting into trouble, and I didn't want to face either of them if they showed up to Terrell's house.

"Tay, don't let them call the cops. And don't tell them where I am, okay?" I asked, but received only silence in response. "Okay?"

He was sniffling on the other end, and I felt bad for upsetting him. "Bro, why you didn't call me. I thought you got arrested or something," he said as his voice quivered.

"My bad, bro," I whispered. "Y'all were playing games, and then I snuck out and smoked with Rel, and we fell asleep."

"I'ma tell Jason to come get you," he said.

"No! I can't come home tonight. They'll know I got high and even Jason will kill me. Just tell them you talked to me and I'm spending the night at Terrell's uncle crib, but that the phone died before we could finish talking. And tell them his uncle said he'll give me a ride home tomorrow," I said.

"Bro, you know that's not gon' fly. And K gon' kill me if he find out I lied for you. I'ma bring the bike!" he said.

"Chill, Tay! He won't find out. Just tell him that's what I told you. Tomorrow, we gon' hit something, but I'll be home right after that," I said.

"Bro, you told me you were done with all that!"

A streak of guilt hit me as he said it, because I knew he was right, and I hated that I was breaking my promise to him.

"Bro…look, um, this it for real. And we just doing one thing and that's it!"

"Don't do nothing stupid, Clay. You already in enough trouble," he reminded me.

"I'll holler at you tomorrow," I told him. I ended the call, knowing he was probably home rehearsing what he was going to tell Kemis and Pastor D.

I was nervous that Jason and Daveon would beat the truth out of him, and subsequently come to Terrell's and do the same to me. Whatever he told them must have worked since he didn't call me back on Terrell's phone all night.

Returning home that night was not an option: At some point while we were smoking that night, we made a plan to meet Jon and Josh at the mall that next day to steal high-dollar items to take to Flip. Josh's cousin agreed to drop us off and pick us up outside the mall so we wouldn't have to worry about transportation, and we could carry out a lot more merchandise. We already knew which store we planned to hit up before we even arrived and had plans to grab as many expensive pairs of jeans as we could and run out to the car.

That next day, I rode in the backseat with my eyes closed while Wood drove us to the mall, feeling tortured with my promises to God that I was done stealing. The guilt inside my chest told me that it would have to be my last time out, and I made one last promise that I was done after I got paid if God would shield me from the police. I then thought about my brothers, who I knew were worried since I hadn't shown up in the morning like I had promised I would. Before entering the mall, I used Jon's phone to call Jason to keep him from worrying.

"Baby bro, where you at?" he yelled after I told him it was me.

"Jay, chill, bro! I'll be home in a lil' bit. We just made a quick stop!" I said.

"You told Tay that Terrell's uncle was bringing you home, and now you on Jon's phone. What you doing? We been waiting on you since this morning, and it's after one!" He was getting louder, as was Kemis, who was in the background yelling and demanding to know my whereabouts and threatening to take the phone from Jason.

"Bro, we on the way!" I said in hopes to reassure Jason not to worry, but it didn't work.

"Clay, you need to come home, bro. K fucked Tay up last night after he found that little rope ladder thing in yo' room. I'ma tell you, if Kemis and Kyle catch you outside before you get here, you gon' wish you had come home. Unc on his way to start looking for you too, and he said he gonna bring some other people from the church. You need to get home and quit causing everyone to worry about you!" he yelled.

"Jay, don't let them do that. Don't let Unc get church people involved! I promise I'm on the way. I gotta go," I said, trying to end the call before he heard anything in the background that could give away my location.

"Don't hang up—"

I quickly ended the call as we were walking inside the store and powered off Jon's phone, knowing that Jason would likely call back repeatedly.

Wood told us he would be waiting outside the doors to one of the department stores, which was where we had planned to lift expensive, name-brand jeans. We did our best to stroll through the mall inconspicuously, learning from our previous encounters. We split up before walking into our target store so security wouldn't immediately begin to watch us when we arrived through the entry doors. We knew to walk casually and pretend like we were checking prices, pretending to be interested in items we knew we wouldn't buy before making our way over to the jeans.

Once we were all in the same vicinity, Josh walked toward the glass doors to make sure Wood was waiting by the curb, and then gave us the signal. We each racked up an armful of jeans so high we could hardly see over them, gusted through the aisles in between clothing racks, and burst through the exit doors of the store as we heard multiple people screaming for us to stop after we activated a security alarm.

"They coming! Go!" Josh yelled. My shoulders shook so hard from his announcement I nearly dropped the pile of jeans, which I could barely contain in my arms.

We scrambled to the car, and all tried to climb in simultaneously after loading the piles of jeans into the trunk. One of the security officers had grabbed Jon by his shirt, and it took Jon kicking, the rest of us tugging on Jon from the opposite direction, and Wood speeding off before the officer lost his grip.

"Shit," Wood yelled. "They gonna get the plates!" He noticed a security truck behind him when he exited the mall lot, and pulled into a nearby plaza and suggested we all get out in case he got pulled over. The four of us filed out of the car and fled as Wood drove from the area.

We ran together through a neighborhood lined with luxury cars and the manicured lawns of large, fancy homes. We cut through backyards and scaled fences, which aggravated loud family dogs before we decided to split up and circle back to a nearby train station.

Just as I turned to head in the opposite direction from the crew, a police vehicle blazed down a lengthy street in our direction, blue and red lights flashing and sirens whirring, and I took off in between two houses and into the backyard of one of them, where I tore my pants at the top of a metal fence before cutting through another yard, finding myself on an unfamiliar street wondering where to go next.

23

ON THE RUN

My lengthy time spent in isolation traveling through unfamiliar residential streets allowed me to reflect on what I had gotten myself into, and wondered if Kemis would ever return my phone, or would he instead just chain me to the bed, or actually send me to live with Pastor D as he had threatened many times before. He had threatened the same to Daveon, who unlike me, had mostly been staying out of trouble.

I wondered if Tay had given up on me and finally broken code and snitched to Kemis and Pastor D, disclosing to them the details of everything I had been doing, and where I was keeping my various stashes of money and spoils. I wondered if he had told them I had amassed enough money to pay the rent and the car note that Kemis had been struggling to pay over the years, or that I had turned my locker at school into a spare closet where I could keep name-brand clothing that I could change into in the bathroom every morning before my first class.

After minutes of running without hearing sirens or anything that sounded chaotic, I slowed to a walk and into a casual stroll, landing at the end of a cul-de-sac where a gravel path awaited. Gray clouds were nestled tightly underneath the sun, and a cool breeze whisked through the wooded area I was near. Had I not been in fear of being captured, I could have enjoyed the scenery of the path that led through a peaceful line of trees, over a small wooden bridge, and eventually out to open, crowded soccer fields lined with parents watching their children bounce around during games.

I remembered being on the fields before and knew that on the other side was a path that led to the train station. Finding another group of trees allowed me a few moments to crouch down and catch my breath before traversing the lengthy corridor of the soccer fields.

I strayed briefly from my path to get water from a drinking fountain before trekking away from the fields. The shouts from the games were replaced with the faint sounds of a train nearing the station. I picked up the pace and ran until I reached the platform just as a train whistled away. I hunched down on a bench with my hoodie pulled over my head to catch my breath, anxiously listening for the sounds of the next train and forcing myself to think about my arrival home and what I would say to my brothers. I hadn't figured out anything by the time a familiar voice called out to me.

"Bruh, what you doing? We gotta roll!"

Across the train platform and on the street in front of the train stop sat Josh in the passenger seat of a different vehicle being driven by Wood, smiling above a lowered window and calling over to me. I looked around and quickly hopped up to join them in the backseat of the car.

"Where y'all get this? And where Terrell and Jon?" I asked once I closed the door.

"You don't wanna know. And them niggas not answering the phone!" exclaimed Josh.

"Damn!" I uttered, hoping my other friends weren't in police custody. I knew the three of us had only narrowly escaped, and felt nervous being with Wood and Josh knowing the police were searching for all of us, and not knowing where the car we were in came from.

I hunkered down in the backseat in silence, trying to recover from the panic of only narrowly escaping apprehension. It made me wonder if God had actually listened to my prayers even though I was behaving so badly. I could barely concentrate on the dialogue between Wood and Josh, and their efforts to fill me in on how they successfully took another car at gunpoint.

"Bruh, Jon just texted," Josh said. "He said he at Flip's crib! Let's ride and then we can drop off this shit! Still don't know where Rel is though."

We rode until we reached the entryway to Flip's apartment complex, a neighborhood where I doubted we could successfully carry armfuls of expensive jeans without getting relieved of them at gunpoint if anyone saw us. Wood, Josh, and I had to double up the amount we carried, as well as the length we had to travel with them since Wood abandoned the car a few buildings down from Flip's unit. Jon was seated outside on the stoop awaiting our arrival, and stood to open the door for us when he saw us turn the corner and walk underneath the stairwell outside.

"Can't believe y'all made it," Jon said while propping open the door.

"Damn! Been waitin' on y'all!" A mouthful of gold shone from across the room when Flip smiled after seeing our spoils. "Ain't nobody ever brought that many fucking pair! How many y'all got?" He asked.

"We ain't count that shit yet! This our first stop!" Josh said.

"Aight put it in there on the bed and I'll look!"

He used one of his bedrooms as a stash room, which he tried not to keep full in case the police ever got into his house. After he went into the room and came back out, he counted out a few one-hundred-dollar bills for each of us for the jeans and a previous drop we had made. He then turned to me and gave me extra.

"Lil' speedy this for that stuff you brought me the other day! You stay keeping me paid. I'ma double you up next time! And when that other lil' nigga get here I'll give him his cut too," Flip said.

"Wait why he get extra? You ain't pay me for that phone I brought you last week yet!" Josh said, looking dissatisfied that I had received substantially more than the rest of them.

"Yo' who da fuck you talking to? That shit you brought was worthless! He brought me some real shit!" Flip said to Josh. I tried not to beam with pride from feeling like I was finally getting the acknowledgment I deserved for my hard work, despite Josh always wanting credit for everything we all did.

The four of us trekked out of the apartment complex where a car parked on the side of a gas station immediately caught Wood's attention.

"Yo, y'all stay here watch me get that shit real quick," he said. He picked up the pace and crossed the street into the lot, looking around to make sure he wasn't seen by anyone inside, and slipped into the driver's seat of the car. Within seconds he was off the lot and picking up the rest of us, with no one even seeming to realize that a vehicle was missing from the lot.

"Did they leave the keys in it?" Jon asked.

"Naw nigga! Remember that video I showed you? You don't even need keys for this kind," Wood said. "Damn this shit is so fucking fast, bro! Record this shit bro!" He handed his phone to Josh who immediately turned on the camera and started filming the dashboard along with Wood's smiling face.

We neared my street after a few minutes of filming and riding, and I knew the last thing I needed was for them to be filming when Kemis saw me arriving home in a stolen car.

"Yo, let me out at the corner Wood! I'll walk the rest," I said. "I'll see y'all Monday."

"Aight C, We'll see you," Wood said.

"Bruh, holla at me tonight. I gotta tell you sumthin'," Jon whispered out of earshot of the others after we had all said our goodbyes and I prepared to step out of the car.

Josh exited from the front seat shortly after I got out, and I assumed it was to give a brief dap or fist bump in celebration of our big pay day.

"I'll see you Monday, bruh," I told him, reaching my hand out.

"Yeah that's cool, but I'ma need like three-hunned off you," he said.

I confusingly thought he was joking, and quickly brushed him off with a laugh. "You crazy, bruh. I'll get at you later."

"Naw…I'm fucking serious! I'm the one that set you up with Flip. You wouldn'ta even known that nigga without me! That shit is mine, nigga!"

Realizing he was serious, I quickly changed my tone. "Yo, you got yo' own bag, bruh. I earned my shit, so what the fuck you on right now!"

"J, we gotta roll and get out this shit, bruh!" Wood yelled from the window, seemingly unaware of what was happening.

"I'm on this, nigga! Give me yo' shit!" Without warning, he pulled his weapon the way he did with a total stranger, but this time pointed it directly at my face. I briefly glanced up and down between him and the two barrels that faced my forehead.

"You just gon' rob yo' boy since second grade?" I asked in a low voice, feigning calmness in hopes that my soft tone would deescalate the scene.

"Josh, what the fuck! Yo, them niggas…" I could hardly concentrate on what Wood was yelling, but I knew he was issuing a warning that we all needed to leave.

Josh and I stared directly into each other's eyes, as though a black metal object with the potential to end my life wasn't staring right back at me. His eyes were telling me more about him than the weapon he was holding could, and I stepped backward with confidence that he had no plans of pulling the trigger. I hadn't realized at the time that I had been surrounded by some who did not hold that same confidence.

"What the fuck you think this is, nigga! You gon' shoot my baby brother like—"

I was quickly hurled to the ground, my knees and elbows catching my fall, when chaotic yelling and successive gunshots rippled throughout the street. I froze on the pavement, unsure if the sharp pain that barreled my knee was a product of the gunfire, and equally unclear how my brothers had managed to blaze through me and scuffle with Josh without either of us knowing they had been around.

"Yo, they coming, bro! We out!" Wood yelled before speeding off in the car without Josh as the sounds of police sirens drew near.

"Get up, bro!" Daveon yelled. "We gotta go!"

Josh was sprawled out on the ground, groaning for help when Daveon and Jason tugged me along by my shirt. We fled through an alleyway and behind another apartment building across the street, running until we reached a spot safe enough to plan our next move.

Jason lifted the lid of a dumpster, and it slammed shut when the sounds of metal clanking down to the bottom echoed inside. "Day, run home and put my car keys on the front porch. Clay, you run to the back of the Quikky Mart and hide. As soon as I can get to my car I'ma get you, aight?"

I ran off alone as I was instructed, accompanied only by an eerie feeling that something was off, and that I wouldn't see my brothers again. I almost turned around to go find my brothers, but didn't want to be caught by the police, and didn't want them to be unable to find me later.

I hobbled over to press my shoulder against the brick in the back of the Quikky Mart building and slouched down to tuck my head and hug my arms around my knees, resting on top of a pile of loose pavement. I wanted more than anything to call my brothers and tell them I was sorry and to come pick me up. I wanted to see their faces more than anything, even if it meant I would catch all of their hands first.

My rest break turned out to be a mistake, as my arms were soon being clinched and tugged by two police officers, who dragged me away while I kicked and yanked with all my strength.

"Stop resisting kid!" one of them yelled while they wrestled me down onto the grass next to a waiting police vehicle.

"This will be a lot easier if you just calm down, kid! We're putting you in handcuffs since you won't stop fighting! You just gonna make it harder on yourself for not cooperating!" the other officer yelled.

I responded with all the obscenities I could muster, bridled only by the grass that crowned the entrance of my mouth. I became winded with the exertion it took to unsuccessfully shield my wrists from the tightly locked handcuffs and went stiff as they lifted me off the ground and placed me into the backseat of the police car.

I kicked the door from the inside of the vehicle after it was slammed shut and continued kicking while I watched an African American uniformed officer, who looked to be the age of Kemis, circle around the vehicle and open up the driver's side door.

"Young buck, I'ma need you to stop kicking my door! If you damage it, they gon' add extra charges, and yo' mama gon' have to pay for it. I'm sure she already gon' be upset enough at you. You don't wanna be in here, then you shouldn't be out stealing!" he lectured after sitting in the driver's seat and shifting the vehicle into drive.

"I ain't steal shit!" I yelled, although I was slightly relieved that stealing was the only charge he mentioned after everything that had just transpired.

"I don't know man. You look like one of the kids on the picture we got from the store security, and another officer saw you on a street near the mall running away from him. Your little friend got picked up too. And they said you all stole some cars!" he said.

I stopped kicking and threw my head back into the seat, having no energy left to fight after learning that the secret was out.

"What's your name?" he asked me after I had calmed down.

"I ain't telling you shit!" I said, emotionally and physically drained and uninterested in his questions, and terrified about what was about to happen and how long I would be in custody.

"Lil' man, come on. You can't be more than ten years old. I know your mama and daddy didn't teach you to be disrespectful like that!" he replied.

"I don't have a mama and daddy," I said, annoyed that he assumed I did.

"You have to have a mama and daddy—it's a scientific fact that you can't be here without a mama and a daddy," he said.

His statement only infuriated me, and worsened my agitation. "You clearly don't know shit about science, cause I don't have either," I replied.

"You gonna have to give me your name kid so we can get you processed, and then you'll be released to your parents."

"I told yo' ass I don't have parents," I said.

"Okay, suit yourself. Do this the hard way," he said.

24

RIGHT TO REMAIN SILENT…OR GET LOUD

The only thing I had been offered was water and applesauce after I had alternated between sitting, standing, and every type of fidget in an isolated holding room they had placed me in that contained hardly anything besides a low-lying steel toilet, a hard scratched up, dirty bench, some wrinkled magazines, and old, discolored books that sat in a plastic chair near the bench. There was a small, dirt-stained window near the ceiling that I wished was a few feet lower so that I could look at something besides the walls and the tiny window in the locked green cell door which I kept staring at in hopes that it would finally open.

I wished it had been more like the jails on television, where I could place my constitutional phone call and tell Tay my goodbyes. I had grown tired of pacing, jumping, and push-ups, and had finally given in to the discomfort of the bench, lying back to stare at the ceiling and imagine what was taking place outside of the walls I was in.

After what seemed like hours of regretting my actions and considering what route I could have taken to avoid capture, and wondering if Jason and Daveon had gotten arrested, I was ordered out and escorted into a room where I faced the glares of Kemis and Pastor D. Had I not been in the hands of officers, I likely would have turned and made a run for it, since seeing them only added to my distress. Across the table from the two of them was the officer that had transported me, a police detective who wore a suit, and an older, gray-bearded black man with thick glasses who stared at me when I walked in.

"You must be Clay. Come on in and take this seat next to your brother. My name is Joey Martin. I'm a juvenile officer and I'm required to be here with you while the police talk to you…"

I stared intently at him as he continued talking since it kept me from having to actually face my brother. Once he stopped talking, the detective started talking, and explained to Kemis and Pastor D everything that led up to my arrest that day. He showed them images from the mall security cameras that depicted me carrying jeans outside and showed them printed images of me getting inside the car.

I tried my best to act as though I was more interested in the bland pictures that canvassed the walls of the room than those the officer had set before us on the table. I had no plans of admitting to stealing anything, even if I had been caught on camera.

After I denied that it was me, denied that I had on the same exact shoes and clothing that I was wearing in the images, and denied knowing any boys by the names of Terrell, Jon, or Josh, the same officer reached into a folder and began pulling out images from previous incidents where the four of us had been out stealing.

"So, our intel detectives believe Clay has been involved in a lot of thefts throughout the area. Most of these happened between eleven o'clock at night and like two in the morning, although some were during afternoon and evening hours. Here are some images from parking lots that were hit, and they believe that's him. Here is an image from another mall incident that happened months back—same four kids, at a cell phone store. Here's another apartment complex parking lot…. here's a mall parking lot…some of these resulted in police chases—this one in particular," he pointed to a picture from the night that Jon got caught, "one of the same boys that he was with today, Jon Davidson, his schoolmate, was apprehended that night. He was the only one caught, even though we have video of four kids involved. A gun went missing on this night from one of the cars.

"One incident became quite serious, as the victim already identified one of these boys as being the one who indicated he had a weapon when the victim tried to stop him and another from stealing out of his car. That's being investigated as robbery! There was another vehicle hijacking that took place shortly after these boys fled the mall. And an additional car reported stolen. Overall, we're talking thousands in cash, stolen credit cards that were later used, very expensive jewelry, cell phones, possibly multiple firearms, and some cars. One of these nights some car keys were taken, and the next day the car went missing. I have a feeling this little ring is bigger than just these four, especially since some guy or guys have been helping them with transportation…Clay, you've been stealing for a long time, haven't you?" he asked.

"No!" I denied vehemently.

"No? Where'd you kids get all this money y'all are posing with?" he asked before flopping down a sheet that contained pictures we had taken in Terrell's bedroom while we were goofing around one night. They showed me displaying a large wad of cash in my hand, as was Terrell, while Jon was pointing a firearm at the camera. I hadn't known at the time the pictures had been posted to social media, or that the police could see the posts. I closed my eyes, wondering why a witty response hadn't leapt into my brain like it did at school when I was under fire.

"He's not answering questions today…We just need to know what to do to get him home. I'm sorry for whatever trouble he put you through today," Kemis told the detective.

I was shocked to hear him speak up after watching him nervously bounce his leg up and down and hearing him sucking his teeth in anger as the officer spoke. I knew that he knew it was me in every single picture, and knew he only wanted to get me home to strangle me. I considered confessing to everything they had accused me of, and adding in my own charges, just to get them to house me for the night.

Pastor D glared at Kemis disapprovingly, as though he was willing and ready for me to offer up a full confession and discuss the thousands of dollars in cash and prizes I was responsible for taking.

"Sir, he put us through a lot with that disrespectful mouth! He's been using profanity since he was in custody and wouldn't even give us his name! Not to mention the kicking the police car and thrashing he was doing. Fortunately, one of his friends told us everyone's names, which was how we were able to finally get you down here!" the uniformed officer who arrested me stated.

I knew Kemis was seething as the arresting officer outed me and my mouth, while I seethed at the thought of one of my friends telling the police my name.

"Clay, there's absolutely no reason to be disrespectful to this officer. He was simply doing his job and deserves a lot more respect and cooperation than what you gave him! These officers risk their lives nearly every time they put on that uniform. It sounds like you owe this officer an apology," Pastor D said, looking at me with expectation in his countenance.

I didn't apologize, but instead rolled my eyes and sat silently, hoping the moment would die naturally. I pressed my back into the seat while Pastor D slid his arm under the table near my thigh and fiercely gripped a lock of my flesh in between his thumb and the side of his forefinger.

"SH—I'm sorry!" I screeched, prompting him to release my flesh back to me.

"You're sorry for what, Clay?" Pastor D asked, looking as though he dared me not to answer.

"For the way I spoke to you," I told the officer, embarrassed that I was being humbled in front of him after having been so obnoxious when we rode in his squad car earlier.

"Before we let you go, there was an incident that happened about thirty minutes before Clay was arrested…he is not a suspect, but we are hoping for his cooperation as a witness," the detective continued.

I closed my eyes and exhaled, as I had assumed up until that point that they hadn't known about it.

"What you mean?" Kemis asked.

"I know he is saying he doesn't know this kid, but Joshua Grayson was shot on the sidewalk on Springdale Road today. Clay, I know you were with him earlier, so I'm just trying to see if you know about any of this," said the detective.

"Wait, is Josh aight?" I forgot that I was supposed to pretend not to know him before blurting the question, but desperately needed to make sure he was alive.

"We don't actually know. He was transported to the hospital—but that's all we know right now," the detective said.

"Clay, were you at a shooting?" Kemis asked with wide eyes.

I used all my effort to mask the fear inside, lowering my eyes and briefly shaking my head to indicate that I knew nothing of what they spoke.

"Clay, you're not in trouble on this. We just need to know what happened," the detective continued. "We don't want any innocent lives impacted, and don't want to go arrest anyone that shouldn't get arrested." He looked and spoke as though he knew exactly what happened, and was merely waiting on me to confirm.

There were too many thoughts colliding with one another in my brain to coherently articulate the sequence of events that led to the gunfire. I knew there was a gun. I knew there had been words—from Wood, from my brothers, from Josh. I couldn't hone in on the chronology of it, and didn't want to. I wanted to erase the day, erase the night before, and be in bed with my blanket pulled over my head. I wondered if Josh was still alive, or if he was lying in a hospital bed fearing an imminent death, and I wondered why Wood drove off, leaving his cousin to die. I had more questions than answers, without the ability to deal with either.

"I don't know shit about shit," was the only answer I could muster since I had once heard it during a police interview on a television show.

Pastor D and Kemis simultaneously sighed, but Pastor D's sigh was abruptly followed with another gruesome pinch to my leg. It was only a foreshadowing of the pain I felt nearly an hour later, but not before the officers had one more word with Pastor D and Kemis.

"Do the two of you mind if I speak with you in the hallway briefly?" the detective asked.

Everyone filed out of the room while I rested my head back on the table, thankful for what I knew would be my final moments of peace and calm.

25

THE RECKONING

"**B**ro I'ma punch you in yo' fucking throat!" Kemis stormed through the doorway of Pastor D's guest room, which had been turned into my bedroom for the day. I had just dozed off after having time to settle into a comfortable bed and refused to willingly subject myself to what I knew was coming.

"Bro, wait! I ain't even do that shit! I was just there 'cause I needed a ride," I lied, having no other words to mitigate his anger. Before I even had all the words out, he was hurling a belt in my direction, not seeming to care about where it landed, and I struggled to determine which body part to try and shield from him. I sprang off the bed in attempt to run past him, hoping to find someone to intervene and save me from my demise, but when my fingertips closed in on the doorknob, he bear-hugged me from behind and flung me to the floor before slapping my head and continuing his belt attack.

"So you wanna steal huh?" he yelled.

"Damn! Ah! No, K!" I protested, trying to pull away from him. He snatched my ankle to pull me towards him before he started hitting me again.

"And got the nerve to stay out all night? You lost your mind! It's cool cause I'm a help you get it back! Get over here!" he ordered after already hitting me multiple times. I kicked my ankle out of his grasp and ran to the other side of the bed, and then toward the window when I realized he was right behind me. None of it stopped the hits from coming as he followed me and fenced me in at each destination.

"Wait, K! Just let me talk!" I begged in between breaths. I tried again to get out of the room, but he overpowered me, threw me onto the bed and yanked me down to the floor. He pulled down my pants and used them to drag me backwards across the rug, burning my elbows that I had planted to try to leverage my escape, and painfully swung his belt on my backside while dragging me and preventing my crawl to safety, screaming at me in between hits.

"You got the nerve—" Whap! Whap! "To be cussing out damn police officers!" Whap! "After fucking stealing!" Whap! Whap! "And staying out all night, stealing cars and shit!" Whap! Whap! Whap! Whap! "And then y'all at a fucking shooting?" Whap! Whap! Whap! Whap! Whap! "Stand up!"

Desperately trying to get away, I managed to flip onto my back and grind my free foot into the carpet to scoot underneath the bed. He scrambled to grab my other ankle and hauled me from underneath the only shelter I could find.

"Kemis!" Pastor D barged into the room and threw himself in front of Kemis, grabbing his arms and backing him away from me, appearing startled by what he saw and heard. "Come on now, son. You can't hit out of anger like this! Clay, lie down and go back to bed…I'll be in here later." He sighed and turned his attention back to Kemis while I huddled in the corner of the bed, hoping Pastor D would keep my brother away from me. "I know he misbehaved terribly, but this is not okay! Let's go!"

He grabbed Kemis' arm and led him out of the room, while I crawled under the blanket, trying to clutch my wounds and stifle what had become an uncontrollable cry.

I found myself enraged with my brother for how badly I hurt, and equally upset with myself for stealing that day, and all the days, and being too stupid to realize that nearly every place we had stolen from was monitored with video surveillance. I wondered how many more charges I would end up facing if they kept reviewing video footage, and whether my juvenile record would result in me walking out a probation period or with me establishing residency inside a detention facility.

I wondered what else my friends had told the officers besides my name, and whether they had outed me as the one in the group that had likely gotten away with the most because of my ability to run away the fastest. But mostly, I wondered would I ever see Josh again, or would I have to face backlash once word of my absence from his funeral spread. I wondered if Jason was okay, and whether he was at home regretting that fact that he had gone out looking for me.

26

JOSH AND JON

The sounds of the bedroom door creaking open brought my somber nap to an end, as I was paranoid that Kemis had snuck back into to continue beating me until I lost feeling in my backside. Instead, I woke up to find Pastor D inching toward a chair nearby. He had a large plate containing a toasted grilled cheese sandwich with grapes and potato chips, along with a cup of water, and had placed them on the table next to the bed. I let my hunger beat out my shame and brought my head out of the blanket in hopes that the food was for me.

"Your auntie made you something to eat. Why don't you sit up—I haven't seen you eat a thing all day. Here," he said as he handed me the plate. I sat up in bed and started scarfing it down as he watched me curiously. "I'm going to ask you something, and I want you to tell me the truth. How long have you and your friends been stealing like this?" asked Pastor D.

I had already felt guilty about my actions and knew he would be even more disappointed in the answer. But he asked in a way that echoed concern and not judgment.

"A while," I said in between chews.

"And how long is a while?" he asked.

"Um, it maybe started like, after Thanksgiving," I responded.

"Why, Clay? I know you know that stealing is wrong. You never know what type of trouble you can cause someone by taking their wallet—they could have had to travel the next day but weren't allowed on their flight because their ID was gone. Did you know one of your friends took a gun?" he asked.

I shrugged my shoulders, unwilling to admit that I had taken guns, one of which I kept in my room for nearly three weeks before deciding to sell it for eighty dollars to a kid from school. The other I sold to Flip for one-hundred and a pair of shoes that I sold to Terrell.

"Did you take any guns?" he asked.

I dropped my chin so low it nearly touched the bottom of my neck. I didn't want to lie to him, so I chose silence instead.

"My word, Clay. What if one of those weapons ends up in the wrong hands. We're seeing little kids take guns to school, or accidentally shoot their friends…even shooting people intentionally! And why are you taking things that don't belong to you? I know you don't have a lot, but you know better, and you know what it's like to be stolen from. I remember when your bike got stolen when it was chained to the fence behind the apartment and you couldn't get around. I know you remember how that felt! What you think these people felt when their things were gone?" he asked.

I shook my head and laid my sandwich back down on the plate, feeling unable to chew or move in nearly any capacity. I knew I had followed my so-called friends into something stupid, and I was mad at myself for it, and somewhat mad at him for not realizing I didn't want to talk about it.

"I mean…" I drifted back and forth in my mind regarding how honest I should be. "Everybody was going in on me for my clothes, my shoes, my haircuts, everything. They say I come to school looking homeless, or say I wear Wal-Mart clothes. They be having everything. They got better phones, and they be dripping with the newest shoes that come out. We can't have none of that stuff, especially after Granny died. I just got tired of being the broke one."

I was tired of being the ugly one, the black one, and the stupid one too, but I didn't feel like I could share all of that.

He sighed and looked around the room. "Clay…I always tell you that you can come to me with anything. Why wouldn't you tell me this has been bothering you instead of letting it get out of hand like this?" he asked.

"I ain't think you would care because one time in youth church you was talking about kids only wanting name-brand clothes and trying to impress our friends on the Gram and thinking everything is about having the latest shoes and stuff," I said.

"I have said things like that Clay, but some of those kids are in a completely different boat than you guys are. Some kids in youth group are well off, and that's all they care about is having nice things to impress their friends. One of the teenagers threw away a pair of two-hundred-dollar sneakers because it had a crease in it! And then other kids have hardly anything but think wearing expensive clothing brings them value. I saw one of our teens at the metro bus stop one day wearing a thousand-dollar purse! It made no sense to me—had she saved money on the purse, she could probably afford a car! So my point was that life is not about having clothes and impressing people on social media because most people's posts are fake anyway! But nobody wants their things to be in so bad a shape that they get teased for it," he said.

He looked at me intently and squeezed my arm. "Listen, when you're in a rough place, you can always call me. You are my family. Your brother told me even when you're on punishment

he let you know you could still call me. I'll come and pick you up.
We'll go eat. We can pick up Caleb and Soph and hang
somewhere. At the same time, you only get one childhood. You
shouldn't be worried about clothes and shoes more than just
having fun with your friends, playing basketball, keeping your
grades up, being a kid. I know there's all this pressure to fit in—
but trust me when I say that sometimes fitting in is the last thing
you want to do.

"God wants his people to be different from everyone else in
the world, to be separate. And if you think about it, a lot of great
people became great because they separated themselves from the
crowd and stood out.

"Look at Kobe Bryant, or Lebron…you think when they
were in high school, they just did everything their friends were
doing? There were probably a lot of times their friends were out
partying while they stayed behind in the gym. Look how it paid
off. Even artists like Chance the Rapper or Kanye West and some
of those other guys. They become famous because they stood out
from all the other rappers, not because they fit in. This is why you
have to be yourself and only yourself…don't let other kids define
for you what is in. You decide! You be the leader, the one who
stands out," he said.

"But Unc, it seem like you have nice things—you always give
us money. Y'all got extra cars…K said you been paying the note
on Jason's car," I challenged.

"Clay, I'ma tell you something. God has given me those
things so I can give to others. But I didn't get any of that illegally.
There are a lot of legal ways to get money—money is easy to find
if you go about it the right way. I can afford name brand clothes,
but most of my shirts are from the Goodwill…I'd much rather
spend my money on a shirt for you than a shirt for me!" he
exclaimed.

I crumpled my face in disgust, imagining him shopping for used clothes, and pictured my friends laughing me out of school for trying the same.

"Do you know what the average life expectancy is for an American?" he asked me, reminding me of science class.

"No," I said.

"Okay, let's pretend that it's seventy-five years. How many years between starting school and graduating high school?" he asked.

"Um I guess about thirteen," I responded.

"Right, so you get thirteen years to go through school, from kindergarten through twelfth grade. Then, how much time do you have left after that?" he asked.

"Um, I need a sheet of paper," I said.

"Seventy-five minus thirteen is what?" he asked.

"Um…it's sixty…sixty-two?" I said, unsure if I had gotten it correct.

"That's right! So, thirteen years of school until graduation, and then sixty-two years outside of that. You wonder why I had you do all that? Doesn't it sound stupid to stress over impressing people you may only see for thirteen years, when you'll have sixty-two years without them? Thirteen years is wayyyy smaller than sixty-two…"

After listening to him, I was even more angry that I had gotten into so much trouble with my friends, just for them to tell the police my name, and for one of them to turn a gun and try to rob me.

"Do me a favor. Can you agree that the next time you find yourself in something like this that you'll call me before you break the law?" he asked.

I nodded my head in agreement.

"I am disappointed in you Clay," he said.

I wasn't sure why those words made me feel so guilty coming from him, especially since I already knew it was the case before he said it. Still, I nearly started crying all over again.

He seemed to sense how I felt and grabbed onto my chin. "But I love you. You know what else? God loves you. Nothing you can do could ever make that stop—even getting arrested and facing charges in family court. He forgives you, but I hope you let this serve as your wake-up call. This is not the life you want…there are other ways," he said.

I was considering his words when someone began tapping on the door, and Kemis slowly opened it and crept in. "Um, hey, y'all," he said awkwardly.

"Hey, son, come on in," Pastor D invited.

"Did you tell him yet?" Kemis asked, as he inched over and joined us at the other end of the bed.

"We didn't quite get to it, but I think now may be a good time," Pastor D responded in a cautious tone.

"Get to what? Is this about Josh?" I asked, after already spending most of the day wondering if the worst would happen.

"Well, yes and no. It sounds like your friend Josh is gonna make it, but he had to have surgery and will probably have another. They don't know when or if he'll walk again. We'll have to remember to pray for him," Pastor D said.

While I was thankful that murder charges were off the table, I knew I had no intentions of wasting any prayers on Josh, except that maybe he go far enough away that I would never have to see him again.

"But apparently your friend Jon, well, he was in a police chase. They thought he may have been involved with Josh's shooting since he was in the car that fled from the scene. He got away for a little bit and then hopped a train and went down to the riverfront. Police down there ended up chasing him since word was out by that time that your crew had been involved in an armed robbery of a car and then a shooting. He jumped in the river to try to get away from the officers that were chasing him," Pastor D said.

"That's crazy! I bet they ain't follow him in there!" I laughed, thinking Jon always came up with the craziest ideas.

"Clay…um….your friend Jon…he didn't come out of that water," Pastor D said softly.

"Yeah, he told us that him and his brother used to go float down the river all the time," I said. "He wild, but I guess not that wild if he got away, and I'm the dumb one that got arrested.

"No…the police… he went downstream…and never came out," Pastor D said.

I looked at him, confused at why he sounded so serious. "He's prolly just hiding, Unc."

"No…he's not. He…they found him…his body. He didn't come out alive," said Pastor D.

I studied his face, waiting for him to keep talking and tell me that he was joking, or that I was dreaming, or that he was talking about someone else. When it became clear he was done talking, I turned my head to Kemis, hoping he would say something to correct Pastor D.

"I'm sorry, baby bro. Yo' boy didn't make it," Kemis added with a whisper.

It was nearly thirty seconds before I was truly understanding their words. I looked again at Kemis, and then at Pastor D before the water slid into my vision. My nasal passages were suddenly too stuffy for my breathing to remain normal, my throat tightened, and the cloud that already seemed to be inside my brain had thickened, to the point where no thoughts seemed to be able to come in or out.

"Ain't no way, bro! They lying! They gotta be ly—"

"The police told us at the station. And I spoke with his aunt. I'm so sorry Clay. I realize this day has had a terrible ending,"

Pastor D added. "I didn't want to lecture you too much about your behavior since I knew we had to talk about this. I'm sure you feel bad enough about everything without having to deal with this…"

They both looked at me like they expected a response, but I had nothing to offer except another round of tears that stung my eyes, along with pain and confusion that hit so hard I could only fall back to hide my head underneath my pillow.

"Clay…can I get you anything?" Pastor D asked.

I responded with a stiff shake of my head, hoping they would both leave my presence. I knew that there was nothing they could give me that I actually wanted.

27

CHANGE OF HEART

Church was the last place I wanted to be that next morning. I thought Pastor D would let me stay in bed considering everything that had happened, but he refused even though I was tired and moody. I had sleeplessly wallowed in depression and anxiety throughout the night, and the previous day's events and my sleepiness weighed equally heavy, prompting me to ignore his demands that I get up and get dressed. After about the fourth time of getting back into bed after he told me to wake up and get dressed, I jolted up after he threatened to get me up the way his mother used to get him up.

There was no youth church that Sunday, forcing us to sit through a boring service during which I took at least three pretend bathroom breaks just to walk around and stretch my legs. I received flirty notes from two girls that sat behind me, which earned me threatening glares from Kemis and from Pastor D. Fortunately, Tay and Jason sat between Kemis and me, keeping me more than an arm's length away from catching a church pinch.

He did manage to reach over them both and thump me during the couple times I dozed off.

But soon after the second thump, a visiting pastor from Atlanta, Georgia took the podium to speak about the Bible in a way I had never heard it spoken before. He said that by the time he was done speaking, he wanted everyone in the room to know where they would be headed after they died. I normally didn't like thinking about death, but I hadn't stopped thinking about it since I had heard about Jon, and the way he discussed the topic had me intrigued. He said he wanted all the younger people in the room to listen closely, especially since so many young men in the black community were dying violently.

The words resonated as heavily as the constant flashbacks I suffered from landing on the sidewalk with my brothers and Josh, and from ducking on the gas station floor with Jason. Moreover, I still hadn't been able to completely process the fact that Jon was no longer with us. When I did think about it, I was zapped with lingering fear, wondering exactly where he was, and if he suffered when transitioning, and if anyone was around, or was he alone and scared. It was strange that when we woke up that morning, we had no idea it would have been Jon's last day on earth, and that it could have been Josh's and mine as well. Had we known it, we would have likely spent the day doing something else, maybe hanging out at the basketball court, playing video games with my brothers, or finding some girls to launch a surprise water balloon attack on.

But even before the most recent encounters, it seemed like every summer break, at least one of us would lose a classmate to gun violence. It seemed like there were more and more police shootings of black people since the one that had taken place in our own neighborhood; some of them had been other kids, which we would hear about on social media. And in our neighborhood, we could often hear gunshots at night, although usually they sounded far away except on New Year's Eve and some summer nights.

The speaker said the Bible was the only book that was "alive," and discussed the Old Testament books of the Bible that had predicted the future, and had predicted the coming of Jesus, and had come to pass. He talked about how most historians, even those from other religions, never disputed the existence of Jesus or the fact that he was sinless and a miracle worker; the only dispute was whether he was the Christ, or anointed one, the son of God. He discussed how archaeological records verified the locations and events from the Bible. He talked about how the resurrection of Jesus was verified by events outside of the Bible. And then he talked about exactly why it was that we could know we were born into sin and why Jesus had to die for our sins to make us righteous.

He said some people in the black community believed that Christ's teachings came from slave masters, but the that the Bible and Christ pre-dated American history and that many people of African descent were believing in Christ long before they came to America.

Some things made more sense to me than they ever had. It made sense that I often felt so guilty when I was bad. I knew that I had done some bad things and needed God to forgive me for them, especially more recently. I felt guilty about Jon, feeling like his family would likely never forgive any of us knowing that it was because of our criminal activity and running from the police that he was no longer here. Reflecting on everything I had been up to left me with a feeling of heaviness and a sense that I knew that God wanted better from and for me.

"The Bible was written by over forty authors in hundreds of years, on different continents. I'll tell you just one thing that convinced me that the Bible was the word of God. The prophecies of Jesus—there are over three hundred prophecies of

Jesus that were written before Jesus was even born. Let me say that again…the prophecies about him were made before he even walked the earth. And when he came, he fulfilled every single one of those three hundred plus prophecies!!" proclaimed the speaker.

I stared at the floor while he continued, his words feeling too weighty to make eye contact, out of fear he would look directly at me and know all my secrets, including the fact that I needed his words. I had never paid that close attention to a sermon before, but the sermon was different because I was hearing it and feeling it inside my chest it at the same time. It was a feeling that brought with it a stillness and a reassurance that despite everything going on, I was okay because of what he was saying. Many of the questions I had about the Bible and Jesus' life and death felt like they had been answered, and for the ones that hadn't been, I still felt an overwhelming sense of peace while I carefully considered each word spoken.

"God is speaking to some people right now to come and give their life to Christ and pray a prayer of salvation. Somebody is saying, 'I don't hear God talking.' It's that still small voice in your heart. It's that yearning you're feeling right now, that urging that you know he is calling you and that you need him—that's God speaking to you. I'm not going to sit down yet because he is speaking to somebody, and I'm going to wait for that person to yield to God," he continued.

A team of singers stood near the front and began softly harmonizing when the speaker asked everyone in the room to close their eyes and bow their heads and asked people to raise their hand if they felt God was leading them to him. It felt like it was me he was talking about, but I was afraid to acknowledge it. I didn't want anyone to know that I was admitting that I had been bad, and that I was in need. I slowly and quietly slipped my index finger into the air, hoping no one would notice.

"Y'all, hands went up all over this place," the speaker said, and people throughout the room responded with shouting and clapping. He asked that everyone that raised their hand up to come to the front of the church. "I know it's uncomfortable, but nobody here is looking to judge you, we just want you to get help and prayer. None of us are perfect…we all need Him."

I didn't want to get up, but for some reason I knew I had to. I stood up and kept my gaze on the front of the room where I had been instructed to go, and was shocked but comforted when Daveon got up too. I made my way toward the aisle, and he was right behind me. He put his arm around me, and we walked together while people on both sides of the aisle we traversed stood and clapped.

The guest Pastor got back on the microphone. "Church family, I know the Bible says the angels in heaven rejoice over just one soul coming into the kingdom. I know they are rejoicing right now. But I gotta say this. It does something to me every time a young black man heeds the call of God on his life. Every life and every soul are equally important in the eyes of God. But between the school to prison pipeline, housing discrimination, the defunding of our education systems, broken families, the mass incarceration of our black men, Satan has used our government to keep our young black men oppressed! They did everything they could to keep black people in certain neighborhoods. They wanted our neighborhoods to remain low income and high crime. They wanted us to have drugs and gangs. They wanted our boys to war with each other and kill each other. They set it up that way! And every time I watch a young black man get saved, I know that God is saying 'Not this one, Satan! Hands off! He's mine now!' And all I can say is thank you God!" he shouted.

The Pastor ended up putting his microphone down and walked over to me and rested his hand on my shoulder.

"Young man, how old are you?" he asked me with a smile.

"Twelve," I told him.

"Wow! I was twelve when God saved my soul as well! Some of us God draws in a little younger. Jesus was about twelve when his family realized he had a special call on his life. You're young in age, but there's a great talent he has given you, and you will use it for his glory. The enemy knows how gifted you are, and he wants you to use your gifts for bad. But God will show you how to use them for him. Tell me something: you been listening and behaving yourself, and doing good at school?" he asked.

I looked away from him, unsure how to tell him that I was a horrible student, an awful brother, and had spent my previous day in police custody. He looked at me as though he wasn't surprised by my silence.

"Young man, the Lord already knows. He has never required perfection from you, and still won't. Even better, he forgives you, and he will continue to forgive you. Would you like to accept Jesus into your heart, and receive that forgiveness?" he asked.

I nodded my head, wondering what he was going to make me do.

"I want you to repeat after me, and then I'm going to pray for you. Is that okay?" he asked.

I nodded, wondering if I would feel saved during the prayer, once the prayer was over, or would I have to wait to feel it until the next day. I wondered if it would help me to stop cussing and lying and sneaking out, even though a part of me no longer wanted to do those again anyway. I listened and repeated the words he told me to repeat, and then he followed up with a short prayer and then talked to me about how important it was to read the Bible and go to church. I thought about telling him how much I hated reading, but I simply nodded my head instead.

"I want you to take this," he said and handed me a card with his name and email on it. "If you ever have questions, need help, or need to talk, you can use this and get a hold of me, okay?" he said.

I don't think I had ever seen Pastor D, who gave both me and Daveon about fifteen hugs each, happier than he had been on that day. And when we all got into Kemis' truck to head home, Kemis continuously wiped tears from his eyes. All he would say was that God was answering his prayers, but I was nervous that he would have higher expectations from me.

28

EXPENSIVE MONEY

Terrell found me near my locker after first period at school the next day, and I wondered if I should tell him what happened at church. Before I had the chance, he filled me in on the latest news.

"Bruh, you hear about Josh?" he asked.

"Unc told me he still at the hospital, but you know I don't have my phone," I said.

"His cousin said he ain't coming back to school, even when he do get out the hospital. They got Wood locked up at juvie 'cause the police said Wood set Josh up to get shot," he said.

"You dead ass?" I asked. "Who they saying shot him?" I asked, curious about what the rumors were and wondering if anyone was fingering my brothers and me.

"They said Josh wouldn't say shit to the cops. I was pissed at first, but I guess I'm glad twelve picked me up when they did. Kept me from being in that drama…or going with Jon…" He paused after he said it, and it seemed neither of us knew how to follow up his statement. "But look, Flip said he had some more money for you 'cause he hadn't paid you for some stuff you gave him a while back. He said he was gon' do it the other day but Josh seemed like he was hatin' on you," he said with a large grin as he handed me eight fifty-dollar bills. My heart sank as I looked at the money, and my hand felt dirty as soon as I took hold of it. I had never felt hesitant about getting money before, but this particular batch of cash felt like it had cost too much.

"Bruh, I shouldn't take this man. I gotta chill out for real," I said.

"Bruh we earned it! You forget all that running we had to do? If you don't want it, take it to yo' brother. You said he lost his job…"

I looked around the hall to make sure nobody saw before stuffing the bills deep into my pocket. Terrell continued, "But look bruh, you should roll out wit' me and Mac tonight. An OG showed him how to get them converters off the bottom of a car, and Flip say he pay like one or two hundo! He said some niggas be bringing like ten a night, and Mac got a hookup on a ride! Want us to come through?"

I could tell he didn't understand the extent that my brothers had me on lockdown. I had gotten no less than two threats from each of my brothers that morning before school, letting me know that it would be a group pounding session if I snuck out of school or didn't come straight home. Kemis had already planned that my next few weekends would be at Pastor D's house, and any night that both Kemis and Jason would have to be out, I was getting picked up by Pastor D curbside at the school. But the main thing on my mind was what we had waiting for us in the family court.

"Bruh, I got court this Thursday! I can't get arrested while I'm waiting on this case," I said.

"I got court too! Still need them bands though," he said.

"*All* my brothers got me on lock. Even Tay said he snitching if I try to sneak out. It's gon' be a minute for me." I made it sound like my departure from the hustle was temporary, but in my heart, I knew it was forever. "Ay, this money will last for a lil' while though!" I said, trying to feign excitement about the money.

"Fa sho…and guess who feeling you now?" he asked, and smiled while he waited for my reaction.

"Lakisha been feeling me dude," I said smiling.

"Naw…Meka said she wanna holla at you."

"Josh's girl?" I asked.

"Yeah! She said she been feeling you for a minute!"

"I can't do that to Josh," I said, pretending to still be loyal to him even though I wanted nothing to do with him.

"Really? Cause he tried to get yo' girl hella times, but she kept telling him no. And Jon had told me a long time ago that Josh the one sent that picture to the principal that got sent to yo' brother, but I ain't believe him! Now I do after I talked to Flip."

"What Flip say?" I asked, in disbelief of what I was hearing.

"He said he ain't trust that nigga Josh, and said we prolly shouldn't either!"

"Dang, bruh…that's crazy. Well, look, I'll text you tonight on Tay phone," I told him, feeling the need to end the conversation quickly so I could process the things he said.

I couldn't believe Josh had been the one to get me into trouble after the party, but after I reflected on the picture Kemis showed me, it was taken near where Josh was standing that night. I wondered if he had also edited it to put the red arrow over my face, or if that was Principal Mack. Either way, the picture came from someone at the party, and I knew he had his phone on him that night. I wondered what would motivate him to see me in trouble with my brother.

I was saddened, thinking how Josh had deceived me into thinking he was happy for me that night, and happy for me during the times when we made money together. I was questioning what his intentions truly were, and disappointed with myself that I had followed someone that had nothing but ill will towards me.

After school, I waited for Tay to walk to the library before I locked the door to the room and dug out all of my money and added in the latest bills I had gotten from Terrell. I had hardly spent any of the funds in nearly a month and marveled at how large my stash had become. My astonishment was soon replaced with guilt, and I wondered if God would be mad if I kept the money that I had worked so hard for. Part of me felt like I should keep it since I had no more plans of stealing and felt like I shouldn't punish myself for past behavior. On the other hand, the thought of spending it produced an uncomfortable feeling, making me want to throw it all in the trash.

I stopped counting money and considered calling Pastor D but then decided against it since I knew I didn't want to tell him the exact details of my predicament. I felt like Tay would tell me I would have to throw it away, but felt like Daveon would tell me to keep it.

I soon felt sick in my stomach, and didn't even want to be around the money, thinking of how I had gotten it by learning from Josh, someone who I should have known better than to trust. I decided I should give it to Kemis since I had caused him to lose out on so much money, but I was nervous about his reaction when he saw how much it was. Even though he knew from our meeting at the police station that I had gone out a lot with the crew, neither he or the police knew the extent of our encounters or how much we had gone out, and I had no intentions of sharing that with him.

I stuffed as much of the cash as I could into a shoebox, and then crept into Jason's room to feel him out about facilitating the transfer, finding him sprawled out on the bed and texting on his phone.

"Sup baby bro," Jason said, barely looking up from his phone after I walked in and closed the door.

"I need a favor…and don't trip. Will you give this to K for me?" I asked and held out the shoebox for him to grab.

"Whoa! So you trying to get him to kick my ass instead of yours? He gon' know I ain't get all this from my shifts at the library!" he said after sitting up to take a closer look at the money.

"Just tell him you've been saving or something! He gon' kill me if I take it to him."

Jason put his phone down, grabbed the money, and started counting it, but grew impatient and stopped after realizing how large the stash was.

"He definitely gon' kill yo' ass…but he needs the money. Unc gave him enough for rent for a couple months though. I'll give it to him," he said after a lengthy exhale.

"Thanks," I told him before turning to go back to my confinement.

"Bro!" he called before I could get out the room. I turned around and looked at him, wondering if he had changed his mind. "You barely talked to me since the other day, nigga. I damn near threw everything away for you!"

I had hoped he wouldn't bring it up, still wallowing in the guilt of getting my brothers entangled in something I shouldn't have been a part of in the first place. I wasn't sure if I needed to thank him, or apologize, or both, but the last thing I wanted was for his dreams to be thrown out the door because he was trying to protect me.

"I figured y'all ain't wanna talk about it," I said.

"It's all good, bro. I don't play about my fucking brothers. Y'all are what's important. Me and you are good, but you better be done with that crew and all this shit, bro!" he said.

"Whatchu mean?" I asked.

"You know what I mean! I'm a little salty I was trying to take on extra shifts at work to try to hook you up, and you were doing all this behind my back, and running with dudes that ain't even looking out for you!"

"I'm done, Jay," I muttered, wishing he didn't have to splatter more shame on my face that I was already feeling covered in. I wished I could tell him about Josh, but was too humiliated to admit how stupid I had been.

"Good, cause K ain't gon' be the only one kicking yo' ass if you do it again. And did you finish yo' homework?" he asked.

I shook my head, slightly wishing I hadn't brought him the money.

"Ain't like you got anything else to do, so go get it done!"

"Damn nigga, aight!" I muttered.

"What you say?" he abruptly looked up and threw down his phone like he was about to throw a punch or two.

"Nothin'," I said.

29

FIXING OUR FACES

"Dat's game bruh, I promise!" I told Jackson after the ball left my fingertips.

"Ain't no way!" he shouted, right before the ball bounced around the rim and slowly fell through the net.

"Told you!" I shouted.

"Damn! Run it back one more time!" he challenged.

"Bruh I been beating you all night!"

"I almost had you in that second game though!" he responded.

The two of us were supposed to be asleep after watching a movie with Caleb in the basement of Pastor D's house that had ended hours before, but instead we started talking, which led to trash talking, which led to challenging each other on the basketball court and tiptoeing outside without waking anyone else. I was certain Pastor D didn't know that when he set so many lights up in the backyard that they would be used for post-midnight basketball games.

"Aight dude, one more game. But that's it 'cause I ain't trying to wake up Unc!" I replied.

"What you think he gon' say?" Jackson asked.

I laughed. "I guess you ain't never been in trouble with him before. He ain't gon' say nuthin' nice!" I told him before picking the ball back up.

"Ay, you never told me how you got all that money and all that stuff you brought me though. My boys was like 'I bet he stole dat shit!'" Jackson said.

"I ain't steal that stuff—most of it I bought!" I said.

"Den where you get money like that?" he asked.

I didn't really want to tell him the entire thing, since the only thing in my brain was what had happened to Josh and Jon, and the fact that I knew Terrell had snitched me out to the cops. He later admitted to me that it was him, but stated he felt like they tricked him into it by telling him that one of his friends had been shot, and another had been killed. He was afraid that if he didn't cooperate, he would get charged with something serious.

"It was dumb, but I stole a bunch of shit wit' my crew. Mostly from cars and shit. But we hit up the malls, took a lot of cell phones—that got us the most. We would take stuff to this dude who would give us money," I replied.

"Yo, you should let me—"

"Fellas!" I was surprised to see Pastor D standing on the back porch wearing a thick, dark robe and looking down at his watch. "It is way past bedtime, and I told you two we have to wake up early. What is going on out here?" he asked.

"Nothing, Unc! We just talking about basketball!" I said.

"And how to break the law and get into trouble with the authorities?" he asked.

"Naw! It ain't like that," I said.

"I know what it is like—I told you fellas to go to bed after the movie went off, and the two of you are outside!" he said.

"Ain't like we doing nuthin' bad," I said.

"You are if you're disobeying, and we have an early morning tomorrow and you need to be asleep. This ain't like at home where you get told one thing and do another—and that goes for both of you. I'm waking y'all up at the time the roosters crow," he said.

"What's that even mean?" Jackson asked.

"For real, Unc," I followed.

"Just know that roosters crow early, and you both will regret the decision to disobey. Get inside!" he said.

We both groaned and moped inside, unhappy that our game was ruined and wondering how roosters crowing would impact our lives in the near future. I couldn't think of a time when he didn't follow through on his word, nor of a time that I wished he had failed to follow through more than that next morning when he dragged Jackson and me out of bed to start community service.

As part of an agreement with the juvenile court prosecutors to drop the charges they had filed against me, I had to complete a hefty amount of community service. And since Pastor D apparently had "connections" with where to complete the service, and since Jackson had gotten into trouble with his mom, he volunteered to take us both to complete service time while we stayed with him for the weekend. We hadn't realized at the time that the movie he let us watch that Friday night was the only fun he intended for either of us to have the entire time.

"Unc, we don't even get breakfast first?" I asked, noticing that he was parking his van in a lot next to a building attached to the children's hospital. I had assumed he would at least let us stop for sandwiches.

"Breakfast is at eight. There's plenty you two can accomplish before then," he said.

"Unc, this ain't cool, why we gotta start so early?" I asked.

"Is it cool to steal?" was his only response.

"I ain't steal though, Pastor D!" Jackson said from the backseat.

"Is it cool to disobey your mother and sneak out at night and get written up at school?" he asked.

"Well actually—"

"Don't say the wrong answer, Jackson," Pastor D threatened.

We remained silent from that point on, from the time we walked into the building from the car and into the room where Pastor D introduced us to our service coordinators, who explained to us the types of things we would be doing. Afterwards they led us to a different room with boxes of toys, books, crayons, and other items with the goal of making three hundred care packages for kids in the hospital before lunch.

We had hoped that Pastor D would at least leave us and return later, but once we watched him find a seat at a nearby table and pull out a laptop to work on, we quickly learned otherwise. He mostly remained silent other than to tell us that griping and complaining would not be allowed. And other than his departure to grab breakfast for us, he was there to remind us of that very thing the entire morning, accompanied with threats of additional service hours for the day.

It was a relief to complete our gruesome morning tasks, which involved standing on our feet and filling hundreds of bags, and Jackson and I were thankful to sit outside for lunch, out of earshot of Pastor D where we could complain about how hungry we had been and how bored we were from our duties. But that was short-lived, and we were once again told to "fix" our faces after finding out we would be loading the bags onto carts and taking them around to kids in the hospital.

"How I'm s'pose to just fix my anger if something gets on my nerves," I asked.

"I didn't say fix your anger, I said fix your face. You've been told what to do, so straighten up your attitude and get ready to go do it. Once this is complete, we leave for the day," Pastor D told us.

Soon the two of us were following two nurses down a long hospital corridor, pushing oversized carts that contained the bags we had loaded earlier. While we desired to move quickly, the nurses stopped outside of each room before we entered to explain a little bit about the kid that we would encounter. We had to wear masks and gloves to enter inside some of the rooms due to illnesses some of the kids were facing. After delivering a few of the care packages, and seeing how happy the simple gifts made some of the kids, I wished I hadn't been grumpy and tried to rush through the job. Some of the kids asked us to stay and play with them as they opened the toys in the package, while others were too weak to play, but promised us they would try to get better so they could have the strength to use them.

I was dealing with a range of emotions as we tried to plaster on smiles before presenting each child with their package, but I was overtaken by shock when we entered a room in one of our final hallways.

"Damn, Clay! What you doing here?" he asked with a confused smile after slowly grabbing the rails to pull himself up in his bed.

I couldn't believe Josh was laid up in a hospital bed, appearing just as sick as some of the kids who were hooked up to machines. He looked much more somber than he had on any of his social media posts, where he bragged about getting shot and saying how people were always hating on him. I desperately wanted to sock him in the face, but I knew Pastor D wouldn't react well when he found out.

"Had to do community service for my case. I thought you was at a different hospital," I said.

He pushed a button on the side of the rails that adjusted his bed and allowed him to lean and rest his back. "I was, but they made me come here for rehab. I might get to go home next week."

"Dat's w'sup!" I replied, unsure if I should try to sound excited for him or not.

"Yeah…but my mama said I gotta turn myself in at juvie when I get out," he told me.

"You two know each other?" one of the nurses stood by and asked while holding Josh's care package that we had prepared. I wanted to rip it out of her hand and toss it out of the window.

"Yeah, dis my boy. We go to school together…at least we did." He drifted off mid-sentence and looked down into his lap as though he was reflecting on our time at school, while I wondered why he had made it sound as though we were friends.

"You really not going back to school?" I asked

"I can't because I can't really walk that good yet. My mama said if I can walk better by summer I might go to summer school, but she don't know," he said. "C, you know, uh…I ain't mean for that shit to go down like that. Wood was on some other shit that day. That wasn't my idea."

I shifted back and forth with my hands in my pockets, and looked away from him while I processed what sounded like his failed attempt at an apology. I knew he had meant for it to go down exactly the way it did, up until when my brothers showed up. I wanted to hit him and disable him more than he already was for suggesting it wasn't intentional.

"You buy you them J's?" he asked, changing the subject after looking down at my shoes.

"Naw. Unc let me pick 'em out for being good," I said.

After a long talk about my behavior, Pastor D told me he was proud of me for giving nearly all my money and things away to Jackson and his family. As a reward, he took me shopping and let me pick a few things out. It was the first time I had been to the mall without stealing in a long time. It was fortunate that we had mostly finished shopping when mall security approached us and told Pastor D that I was banned from the mall for one year and asked us to leave. They told him that they had recognized my face from security footage, and that if I came back I would be arrested for trespassing.

"Damn, bruh! I'd be good all the time if mine did that for me! You musta upped your sneak-out game," Josh joked.

"Nah, I'm done sneaking out." I said. I didn't know how to summarize all of my reasons, but the fact that he had nearly caused my brothers to be caught in my mess was a big one.

"Well boys, I hate to cut our visit short, but we have to finish these deliveries," the nurse told us.

"I hate this place, bruh. I hope you off punishment when I get out," Josh added dryly.

"I won't be! Either way my brothers ain't gon' let me hang witchu. We don't fuck with you; and don't try to fuck with us," I said as a warning before walking out and joining the others in the hallway.

30

FAMILY MEETINGS

"**B**ro, we can't under no circumstances tell K. You know how long he been threatening to move us in with Unc? If he find out he gon' make us pack, and I can't live with Unc strict ass!"

Daveon had given his best pitch for why we shouldn't come clean to Kemis about what happened to Josh. On the other hand, Jason thought we would have no choice. We had all heard rumors that someone had dropped Jason's name to the police and that detectives would be coming to arrest him soon.

"Why they even care when Josh ain't talking?" I asked.

"He might not be talking but that don't mean his mama don't want the cops to arrest someone," Daveon said. "Dude might be paralyzed for good!"

"Bruh…I just don't see this ending without us needing an attorney. I heard Wood talking so he can get them to drop his charges," Jason said.

"He ain't even see the whole thing bro! Besides, ain't like you *tried* to shoot this dude. All you did was try to get his gun. He was trying to get you!" Daveon said.

"Yeah bro, but ain't no cops gon' believe that story. Josh ain't gon' tell them that!" Jason said.

"Josh ain't, but Wood might," I said. "Or Josh may just lie and say he wasn't doing anything and y'all just rolled up and got him! Jon woulda told the truth, but they know they ain't gotta worry about him…"

"Wood ain't talking, bro," Tay said.

"Yeah, but how you know?" Daveon asked.

Tay sighed. "Don't get mad, but I went and talked to Wood when they released him. Him and Josh still beefing because Josh thinks Wood is gon' snitch him out to the cops."

"Tay, when you do all this? And why you talking to that nigga?" Daveon asked.

"I had to make sure he wasn't no snitch! And I told him he bet' not say shit else to the cops!" Tay said.

"Wait, Tay, bro. You threatening him and shit? You gon' get some shit started," Jason said.

"Naw, we good. I just ended that shit. I told him if he say shit he done," Tay said. We all turned to look at him in disbelief. "Besides, Josh made enemies all around the block by breaking into people cars in his own neighborhood. He ain't got nobody here but Wood, and Wood ain't got nobody but Josh. Don't be mad, but I went back to that dumpster y'all told me Jay dropped the gun in, and when I went to see him I took it with me to make sure he saw it. Then I wiped it off and put it back when I was done."

Jason's jaw dropped. "Bro, you dropped it back in the dumpster? What if someone saw you?" Jason asked.

"Ain't nobody see it. I snuck out and did it when everyone was sleep," Tay said.

"Tay," Jason stood up and began to crack his knuckles. "I'ma kick yo' ass bro!"

"Wait Jay!" Daveon yelled and got up to hold Jason while Tay got up and scrambled across the room to escape.

"Bro, for real, what was I s'pose to do? Let the police arrest you when you ain't really do shit? If yo' school found out they could take yo' scholarship! I had to shut that shit down! And I don't want you to go away to school, but I wasn't gon' let them fuck up yo' whole life! All Granny wanted was to see you go to college and play! You know K would lose his shit bro!" Tay said, hoping to convince Jason not to pound him.

"Hey, what's all the commotion in here?" Pastor D asked. He, Sister Robin, Caleb, and Sophie had come by to have a taco night and hang out. He walked in, looking confused to see Tay backed up against the wall, while Daveon was a few feet away attempting to restrain Jason. Kemis walked in shortly after Pastor D to see what was happening.

"Um, I wore one of Jay's shirts without asking," Tay said. It was one of his better lies than normal, but still poorly executed since he could hardly make eye contact when he said it.

"Tay, you just gon' lie like that?" Kemis asked. "Jay, what's going on for real?"

We all turned to look at Jason, wondering if he would violate the no-snitch policy now that he was eighteen.

Jason looked over at Tay and frowned. "Not only did he take my shirt, he took the rest of my condoms!" he said. I nearly had to hide under the cover on Daveon's bed to keep from laughing. While Daveon and I were slightly amused that Jason did the next worst thing to snitching, Kemis and Pastor D weren't finding it funny at all.

"What? Dontay, do we need to talk?" Pastor D asked.

"He need a long talk Unc! He snuck out to use them too!" Jason added, prompting Pastor D's eyes and mouth to widen even more.

"Bro for real? Unc, he ly—man…" Tay started to talk, but knew it was best to go along with Jason's lie and take the lecture, as opposed to come clean on what was really happening.

"Dontay, we are going to have the longest talk of your life tonight. You boys get downstairs; the tacos are ready!" Pastor D said.

"This dude told me he was a virgin," Kemis mumbled as he left out of the room behind Pastor D, shaking his head.

"Bro seriously?" whispered Tay after Pastor D and Kemis were gone.

"Hope they get yo' ass. You can't be doing this shit, bro," Jason said as he walked out.

Pastor D had told us earlier in the day that they had plans to come over and have a family meeting with us, and we all settled in around the kitchen table after Kemis helped Caleb and Sophie take their plates to the couch.

"How your service go yesterday, lil' bro?" Kemis asked after sitting down next to Sister Robin.

"Man, how many more hours I got? I don't wanna do it anymore. That shit—I mean, it's lame, bro," I said.

"Watch your mouth, young man," Pastor D said.

"What was so bad about it? Unc said you just packed and delivered packages to sick kids!" Jason said.

"Yeah, but some of them was really sick, like so sick they couldn't even play with the stuff. Some couldn't really use their hands; they was on machines. We hardly got any breaks, and then nobody told me Josh would be there. And it took alllll day! And Unc ain't let us do nothin' fun afterwards!" I said. Jason and Daveon glanced at each other at the mention of Josh.

"Clay, the two of you were both on punishment. I said y'all could go outside and play basketball," Pastor D said.

"Yeah, but when we took the bikes to the basketball court we got in trouble!" I said.

"Because I told you both to stay in the backyard, and you both disobeyed. And then you set a bad example with the language you chose to use and were allowed to complete a dictionary assignment," Pastor D said.

"He was *allowed* to complete a dictionary assignment, Unc?" Daveon asked with a chuckle.

"Yes, allowed, as opposed to what I was about to do to him," he said.

"Clay, I deliver a lot of orders to that hospital. Seeing those kids had to make you feel at least a little bit thankful that you're healthy. I ain't thrilled that you saw Josh, 'cause some of these kids act like getting shot is a badge of honor. I heard he still ain't walking!" Kemis added.

"He not…he gotta do rehab to help him walk," I said.

"That could'a been you, baby bro! Can you imagine possibly never hoopin' again? And I bet it was over some dumb stuff," Kemis said.

"That's a good point, Kemis. And Clay and I had a talk this weekend about how we can help him improve his behavior. Here's what I came up with—every week that you don't get suspended, or detention, or written up, and you don't talk crazy to your brother, no phone calls from the teachers or principal, you do your chores, and here's the big one—you don't sneak off to the basketball court without doing your homework, if you do those things, I'm giving you fifteen dollars each week. We will do this for the rest of the school year, and then we'll renegotiate the terms for summer. That will allow you at least sixty a month, enough to buy yourself something," said Pastor D. "And if you want extra there are always people at the church looking to pay for help around the house."

"Baby bro lil' bad tail 'bout to still be broke," Daveon said, prompting him, Tay, and Jason to all start laughing.

"Day, I want the three of you to encourage him to earn the money, not to discourage. This is about accountability. So, if y'all see him about to leave out without his homework done, say something to him," Pastor D told Daveon.

"Unc, I be telling him all the time to do his stuff. He don't listen to nobody but you," Daveon said. I hated when they talked about me as if I wasn't there and scooted my seat back to get ready to leave.

"No, Clay, we're not done, so have a seat. This isn't to embarrass you. This is to offer you a temporary incentive to get you on the right track. But part of getting on the right track is to acknowledge the fact that you have misbehaved, as well as the repercussions of some of that. Your behavior has caused a lot of issues. Kemis hired an attorney for your case, which costs a lot of money, but thankfully you have what looks like will be a favorable outcome once you complete your service hours. And fortunately, we were able to find Kemis a job, so at least we're over that hurdle. I know you feel bad for the trouble you caused, but you need to make it up to your brothers by showing them changed behavior," said Pastor D.

"Yeah, that change hasn't happened yet. I got an email this past week from his teacher about his mouth still," Kemis told him. I rolled my eyes at his ability to snitch without any shame, especially since it had been my first time in trouble at school for a while.

"Mmmm. That's unfortunate Clay. Start forwarding me those emails…and drop him off at my house next time he's cussing around his teachers. And now we're moving on to Day," Pastor D said grimly, leaving me to wonder what would happen at his house if I did slip up at school. I had no desire to spend any more days with him if it involved a dictionary.

"I ain't been acting like him!" Daveon said.

"Thankfully, you haven't as of late. Your behavior has improved drastically over the past ten to twelve months. But your brother said you missed your curfew again last night—there seems to be a pattern," said Pastor D.

"Oooh," Jason taunted.

"Not by that daggone much!" Daveon defended.

"Bro, you came an hour after curfew!" Kemis clarified.

"That's a lot! And you didn't take his phone?" Pastor D asked Kemis.

"Oh my God," Daveon groaned.

"Stop that. And I heard you've been hanging out places you're not supposed to. And I'm confident that you are capable of improving your grades. So, I'm going to make a similar deal with you. You cannot miss your curfew, as in not even by a minute," he said.

Daveon placed his elbows on the table and leaned his face into his hands. "I don't even want this money," he mumbled softly, causing Jason, Tay, and I to crack up, and Kemis to pop him in the back of the neck.

"Stop, Kemis. Not only do you have to make curfew, but you also have to leave your location turned on, at all times, every single day. As far as your grades go, no less than Cs are allowed. You do all this, since your sixteenth birthday is coming, I told Kemis that I would pay for your car insurance monthly, and I personally would put money on this gas card every month so you can get around." He pulled a pre-paid gas card out of his pocket and slid it across the table to Daveon, who had removed his hands and stared down at the card with his eyes and mouth opened wide.

"Wait, no cap?" Day asked.

"Not even lying. But if you don't fulfill your end, I will let your insurance lapse," Pastor D said.

"And you know you ain't driving without it!" Kemis added.

Jason spoke up and broke the silence. "These some sweet deals, Unc. Now that you checked the bad kids, I gotta question."

"Wait one minute. The bad kids?" Pastor D asked.

"C'mon Unc, we know what it is," said Jason.

"Jay, let me ask you something. What's the legal drinking age?" Pastor D asked.

"Gotti!" Daveon yelled, causing everyone except Jason to chuckle.

"I see what we're doing," Jason said while leaning back in his chair.

"Good. The point is, it's time to turn some things around. It's one thing to not snitch on your brothers—it's another thing to stand by when you know they're acting up," Pastor D said.

"You right, Unc. I shoulda done more to keep Clay outta trouble. I definitely regret it now. And I ain't even gon' be here like that in a few months," Jason said.

"True, but then Daveon can step up to help. It will be sad for you to go, but I'm excited about dropping you off at school. You know I got to get there and pray and make sure no ungodliness goes down in that dorm room!" he expressed.

I hated when they talked about Jason leaving, even if his final departure would be months away. I had not forgiven him for the fact that he hardly gave any attention to any of the local schools, despite multiple calls from the coaches. I was also mad at Kemis, who had practically pushed Jason out of the door and insisted that he leave town, which I did not understand since Jason provided us with so much practical help.

"You shoulda been praying over his room here, Unc," Kemis said.

"And Tay's too, apparently," Pastor D said with a swift glance over to Tay.

Our discussion was interrupted with a knock at the door, prompting Tay to get up from the table.

"That's probably my boy bringing my game back," Tay said as he headed toward the front door. "Who is it?" he yelled through the door.

An unintelligible voice spoke from the other side of the door and I turned back to the chatter that had resumed at the table. Soon Tay returned with an envelope with my name on it.

"Who this from?" I asked Tay, hoping it was from Lakisha.

"Tiger, that dude that's always at the basketball court, said his uncle asked him to give it to you," Tay said with a shoulder shrug.

I opened to find a small note on a folded piece of lined paper that looked as though it had been crumpled before being folded and stuffed into the envelope.

Reading the contents of the note did not provide the clarity I needed regarding its sender:

"Clay. Tell your brothers I live above the dumpster. I saw what they did. If Kemis doesn't give me the money he owes me, I will go to the police.

—R.D. Merryweather"

Everyone became silent, waiting for me to read the note out loud.

"Yo, who is R.D. Merryweather?" I asked.

Jason and Kemis looked at each other with matching expressions of panic, while Pastor D put down his fork as though he wasn't sure what to do next.

"Lemme see that," Kemis said, reaching across the table for the note. He read it and threw it onto the table, and looked at Jason before turning to me. "Clay…I forgot to talk to you about your dad."

"Kemis, you were supposed to already have this talk with him," Pastor D said.

Kemis bunched his lips together briefly before talking. "I know, I know, I just put it off and then forgot!"

"Forgot what?" I asked impatiently.

"Forgot to tell you who he was…and now he's reaching out…that's his name on that note," Kemis said.

By this point, everyone had turned their attention from me to Kemis, waiting for more answers.

"But you haven't said why he thinks you owe him money," Pastor D said.

"Right!" Jason followed.

"Okay, okay, wait. I'll tell you everything you need to know after y'all tell me what he's talking about. What did he see at the dumpster?"

Acknowledgements

As with everything else I do, this page will be quite unorthodox. It wouldn't be possible to acknowledge everyone that deserved it in one page. In fact, I could write at least a page on each person mentioned, and many who are not. I'll do my best to give credit where credit is due, starting with God in heaven who gave me first the Savior, and then a brain, stories, and hands that can type. He also gave me people that taught me and encouraged me during this journey. He gave life and breath and boldness to Harriet Tubman, Dr. King, Malcolm X, and many of those who have gone before us…those who fought for the physical and mental freedom of black people, and those who died as martyrs for that cause. Not enough is being said or done to keep your legacy alive, but I only hope to honor it by shedding light on the fact that your sacrifices changed the world for generations to come, and by acknowledging that there is still more work to be done.

A host of editors and beta readers, to include Darriel Tanner, Cyrus 13, SarahMaew, and J. Flowers-Olnowich, thank you for the feedback.

To all the youth pastors, especially mine, you sowed seeds, gave kids a listening ear that didn't have one, did your best to guide and teach young minds, and consistently sacrificed time and money—a lifesaver, a queenmaker, a kingmaker—thank you. But Dr. Robinson, Pastor Chris B., and Dr. Nyemba did the same. To my high school English teachers and high school coaches, thank you for your long-term service to education and to children that many gave up on. Drs. Fallon, Landry, McParland, Chawla, Oleka—thank you for being awesome educators and training me and my peers how to think, challenge, question, argue, and explore in a more productive manner.

To the Normandy Middle School security guards that chased us down the hallway, and to the one that dragged me out of class—you did too much. To the ones that helped and encouraged, thank you. To Ms. Cooper, I'm sorry.

Professors Barnhizer, and Cook, and Staszewski, Michigan State law professors who I am still afraid of, thank you for challenging me, and showing me that I was capable of more than I realized.

To Kojo, Eugene, Christa, and Craig, mentors and masters in the mind body game, you have done so so much…more than I can express. Thank you for being vessels and constant sources of encouragement. I am a better person because of you.

I have an awesome group of friends that have supported me tremendously. I am unable to name them all here, primarily out of fear of not saying enough, but I'm hoping to focus in more on them when I am able to release my next book in this series.

To my circle of trust, my friends and family, the Bulls, Joneses, Onishiles, Littletons, Stubblefields, Porters, Tanners, Fergusons, G Phi G sisters and brothers, BSU sisters and brothers, Journey sisters and brothers, thank you for being you and for your limitless support of everything I've done.

Special shout out to Choo Choo, Moonie, and Goo, my little talented and spectacular loves. I am inspired by you daily, and praying you continue to seek God, learn your purpose, and walk in his will for you. To the mighty man of God, Charlton, you've done it all. I am my best self only when I have you to balance my crazy. One thousand thank yous.